The Jerry McNeal Series

Chosen Path

(A Paranormal Snapshot)

By Sherry A. Burton

Also by Sherry A. Burton

The Orphan Train Saga
Discovery (book one)
Shameless (book two)
Treachery (book three)
Guardian (book four)
Loyal (book five)

Orphan Train Extras
Ezra's Story

Jerry McNeal Series
Always Faithful
Ghostly Guidance
Rambling Spirit
Chosen Path
Port Hope

Tears of Betrayal
Love in the Bluegrass
Somewhere In My Dreams
The King of My Heart
Surviving the Storm
Seems Like Yesterday
"Whispers of the Past," a short story.

The Jerry McNeal Series

Chosen Path

By Sherry A. Burton

The Jerry McNeal Series: Chosen Path
Copyright 2022

by Sherry A. Burton
Published by Dorry Press
Edited and Formatted by BZHercules.com
Cover by Laura J. Prevost @laurajprevostphotography

ISBN: 978-1-951386-20-7

For more information on the author and her works,
please see www.SherryABurton.com

To my Husband, AKA Tour Manager and Self Proclaimed Roadie, thanks for all the heavy lifting!

To my hubby, thanks for helping me stay in the writing chair.

To my mom, who insisted I keep the dog in the series.

To my editor, Beth, for allowing me to keep my voice.

To Laura, for EVERYTHING you do to keep me current in both my covers and graphics.

To my beta readers for giving the books an early read.

To my proofreader, Latisha Rich, for the extra set of eyes.

To my fans, for the continued support.

Lastly, to my "voices," thank you for all the incredible ideas!

Table of Contents

Chapter One

Jerry's inner radar tingled, letting him know he was no longer alone in the room. Gunter tilted his head toward the far wall and wagged his tail – at least whoever had joined them appeared to be friendly.

Jerry rolled his neck – the guest room was getting a bit too crowded for his comfort. He addressed the unseen entity. "Give me a minute to finish packing and you can have the room."

Though he couldn't see the ghost, the hairs on his arms told him when the spirit moved closer. Gunter didn't seem concerned. Jerry wasn't sure if it was because the dog himself was a ghost or merely because his protector didn't perceive a threat.

The energy changed and Jerry felt the slightest pressure of a hand caressing his face. In an instant, he knew the person was his grandmother. Jerry felt her love coursing through his body as he leaned into her touch. He started to tremble. It was all he could do to hold his feelings in check. *Keep it together, Marine.*

Jerry closed his eyes and saw the woman standing before him. She looked just as he remembered, with heavy wrinkles and eyes that looked as if they could see his every thought. She was staring at him, her aged face creased with concern. Jerry swallowed as tears trickled down his cheeks. *I've missed you so much, Granny.*

She moved her lips, but Jerry couldn't hear her words.

I know you are here, Granny. I can feel you.

Keeping her hand against his cheek, she placed her forehead to his. It was something she'd done when he was little – a game of sorts where she'd send him a message, and he would repeat what she'd said. As Jerry's abilities grew, he found they no longer had to be touching for him to receive her messages. He'd never told anyone they could speak without words. Until this moment, he'd completely forgotten they could communicate this way.

You need to go home, Jerry; she needs your help.

Jerry had no problem hearing what his grandmother said. He just didn't know what it meant. *She who?*

His grandmother continued without answering. *You are capable of so much more than you give yourself credit for. You've been running from your destiny for too long. If you're going to continue on this journey, you must heal old wounds. You must understand this gift you have is your legacy.*

Her saying he had a gift and legacy to fulfill wasn't anything new. His grandmother had always told him he was placed on this earth to do amazing things. Jerry had once reminded her that she too had the gift and asked her what amazing things she'd done. She'd merely smiled and told him, *I'm here to help you understand your gift.* But she hadn't, not to his satisfaction. He'd always felt the gift she touted to be more of a burden than a gift. He was different from all his peers, and in turn, many treated him like an outcast. *Some gift. More like a damn curse.* Jerry opened his eyes, expecting to see his grandmother standing there, and the moment was lost. He closed them again and got nothing. *Damn. She's gone.*

Jerry doubled his fist, intending to send it through the wall, then remembered his surroundings and ran his hand across the top of his head instead. Gunter disappeared from the bed and reappeared directly in front of him. Jerry knelt to scratch his ghostly companion on the head. "Why is it I can see and feel you and yet I can't see my grandmother?"

Gunter yawned.

Jerry patted the dog on the side. "Good talk. Sorry to have bored you."

The door rattled, followed by a loud meow. Before Jerry could stop him, Gunter raced across the room and stuck his head through the center of the bedroom door. Jerry heard Cat hiss and saw Gunter's tail wag from the headless body inside the room. Gunter pulled his head back through the door, looking rather pleased with himself.

Jerry looked to the ceiling. "Of all the people on the planet, you thought this should be my life."

Gunter growled a soft growl.

"I do like having you around. I'm just trying to figure out the why of it."

Gunter lowered to his haunches and watched the door.

Jerry placed the last of his belongings in his seabag, folded the flaps, and clipped it shut. He hefted the bag over his left shoulder then grabbed the duffle bag that held his small arsenal. Jerry started for the door, stopping to give the room a final scan. Gunter joined him at the door and Jerry held out his palm to stop him. "Not so fast, dog. Just because we're leaving doesn't mean you get to use the door."

Gunter gave a small woof.

"You've already scared Mr. Meowgy enough for one day."

Gunter cocked his head to the side.

"Yeah, I know the name's lame, but they thought he needed a better name than Cat."

Gunter licked his lips.

"No, you can't eat him." Jerry doubted the dog would eat the cat, as the only thing he'd seen Gunter eat was a bloody bone he'd brought with him from the other realm. Still, the cat was frightened of his ghostly K-9 companion, and Jerry didn't want to take any chances of further upsetting the animal.

Gunter grumbled a doggy grumble and disappeared.

Jerry opened the door and made his way downstairs. Savannah and Alex were sitting at the kitchen table and looked up when he entered.

Savannah was still wearing her pajamas and hadn't bothered to do anything with her hair. She pointed to the stove. "There's oatmeal in the pot."

"I'm good."

Alex nodded to the coffee maker. "At least have a cup of coffee before you leave. It's already good to go. Just close the lid and hit the button." She was in uniform, and Jerry was happy the sight of it didn't set off any warning bells.

"Don't mind if I do." He shrugged off the seabag, set the duffle on top, then walked to the counter and pushed the button.

Savannah frowned. "I can't believe you're leaving before the Derby."

Jerry turned and leaned against the counter while waiting for the coffee to trickle down. "My work here is done."

Alex laughed. "You may not want to be a superhero, but you sure sound like one."

Jerry shook his head and turned to get his coffee. "I just meant I want to get going before I key on something else."

Alex nodded her understanding. "We're both

grateful for everything you've done for us. I don't know how we'll ever thank you."

Jerry directed his comment to Savannah. "Just answer the phone if I call."

Savannah smiled. "I'm glad you're figuring out you don't have to do this on your own."

Jerry knew she was speaking of his ability to know when others were in danger. Not that knowing meant he could stop whatever it was from happening. He ran a hand over his head. "If it weren't for Max—"

Savannah cut him off. "We owe Max a debt of gratitude as well. But don't go beating yourself up. I didn't pick up anything when Alex was in trouble. You were the one that knew something was going to happen. If you hadn't picked up on the danger, Max wouldn't have been able to help you. It's okay to appreciate the help she gave, but when you're giving out credit, don't go dealing yourself out of the mix."

Jerry took a sip of his coffee. "The main thing I've learned this week is it's okay to ask for help."

Savannah lifted her glass of orange juice. "I'll drink to that."

Alex's phone chimed. Her eyes grew wide as she read the message.

Jerry peered at her over his coffee cup. "Problem."

"My supervisor said the captain wants to meet you and your dog."

"Let me guess: he wants to offer Gunter the keys to the city."

Alex looked from him to Savannah and back to Jerry again. "Are you a mind reader now?"

Jerry laughed. "No, Seltzer told me yesterday. Your captain sent him an e-mail along with the photo of Gunter. I thought maybe Seltzer was exaggerating, but I guess not. Another reason for me to head out."

Alex looked at her phone once more, then set it aside. "So, what's next, you just drive until something calls to you?"

"That was the plan."

"You don't sound too sure anymore."

Jerry glanced at Savannah, who was being conspicuously quiet. "Is she here?"

Savannah looked to the side for a moment, the slightest of smiles crossing her lips. "She is. She said you can feel her."

"I can. I felt her when I woke this morning." Jerry blew out an exasperated breath. "I heard her briefly. But I've got nothing now."

"She seems to think you're trying too hard. Or that maybe you've forgotten how to communicate with the dead."

Alex ran her hands over her arms. "You two are creeping me out."

Savannah placed her hand on Alex's hand. "Don't worry, she's harmless."

Alex looked about the room. "She who?"

"Jerry's granny."

Alex blew out a sigh. "Of course."

Savannah touched Alex's hand once more. "Granny said to tell you she's sorry for imposing. Jerry, she says it's important for you to go to the family reunion."

"She told me the same thing this morning." Jerry rinsed his cup and set it in the sink. "She told me someone needs help. Who does she mean?"

Savannah frowned. "Granny said she can't tell you that. She's changing the subject – wants to know why you don't want to go."

Jerry raised an eyebrow. "You mean besides Uncle Marvin?"

"She said to be nice."

"I am being nice. I can't help that Marvin is her brother. I can't stand the man."

"She wants to know the real reason you don't want to go."

It's too early in the morning for this. "It hasn't been the same since Granny died." Jerry turned to where he assumed she was standing. "You were the only one I ever enjoyed talking to. You were the only one who ever understood me."

"She told me to tell you she will be there. She also said you must go." Savannah's brows wrinkled. "She said it's important."

"It's a freaking family reunion. I've been away

so long, I don't even know most of the people who will be there."

Savannah turned to him once again. "Jerry? How long has it been since you've seen your family?"

Jerry rolled his neck from side to side. "A few years."

"Granny is saying it's been longer than that. She says you haven't been back since her funeral."

Alex went to the coffee machine and put in another pod. "Don't you miss your parents?"

Savannah smiled. "Alex comes from a big family where no one can do wrong. I swear, every time I go over there, I expect someone to break out singing 'Kumbaya'."

"My family is far from perfect." Alex scoffed.

"Compared to my family, yours are the Waltons. Seriously, Jerry, look in the dictionary under perfect family, and you'll see a photo of Alex's entire clan."

Jerry ran a hand over his head. "The problem with my family isn't them. It's me. I'm the one who doesn't fit in. I never have. That's where Granny came in. She was always there to run block for me. Only there's no one to do that now. If I go, I have to face them all on my own, and I'm not sure I'm willing to do that just yet."

Alex returned to the table. "If not now, when? At the next funeral?"

"Jerry?"

Jerry glanced at Savannah.

"Your Granny says it's important that you go. She keeps repeating it. I know it's your decision. But I think you should go."

Alex looked at him over her cup. "Where is home?"

Jerry sighed. "Parked in your driveway."

Alex raised an eyebrow. "Where do your parents live?"

Jerry glanced at Savannah. "Florida."

"Jerry and I have already done this dance," Savannah interjected. "His parents may live in Florida, but that is not where the reunion is."

Jerry sighed. "My parents live in Florida, but the reunion is to be held at my uncle's house near Newport, Tennessee. That's where I grew up."

Alex pushed off from the table, rinsed her cup, and placed both hers and Jerry's in the dishwasher. "Newport?"

"A town about thirty miles from Gatlinburg near the North Carolina state line."

Alex glanced at Savannah, then back to Jerry. "We know where it is. We have a cabin between there and Gatlinburg. It's just a small one-bedroom, but you're welcome to use it if you want. It would give you a bit of privacy if you don't want to stay at your uncle's place. Unless you'd rather stay with your family."

That was the last thing he wanted and the main

reason he wasn't looking forward to going to the reunion. Spending time with his uncle was one thing. Staying in the man's house and having to listen to his lies for longer than necessary was more than he could handle. "If you're sure it wouldn't be a problem, I'd be happy to take you up on that."

Alex walked across the kitchen and pulled a key from the drawer. "Our casa is your casa. Use it for as long as you like. Just let us know when you leave and I'll have the cleaning lady come in."

"At least let me pay for the cleaning." Jerry reached for his wallet and Alex waved him off.

"We're good, Jerry." She handed him the key. "Just put it on the counter when you leave."

Savannah circled the table and hugged Jerry. "Thanks for everything."

"Just doing my job."

She kissed him on his cheek. "Yeah, well, keep doing it; you're pretty good at it."

Alex extended her hand, then reconsidered and moved in for a quick hug. "You're alright, McNeal."

Jerry clapped her on the back then pulled away. "You're not so bad yourself, Alexandra."

Alex laughed. "Don't call me that. And don't tell anyone, or it will ruin my reputation."

Jerry pocketed the key. "It would probably help if I had an address."

Alex retrieved her phone and thumbed the screen. "I just texted it to you."

Jerry turned to grab his seabag and saw Cat sitting on top, sniffing the duffle bag. He bent and lifted the orange tabby into his arms, mindless of the cat hair he'd spent so much time avoiding. Cat purred as Jerry ran his fingers through the feline's fur. It was incredible that the simple act of bringing a cat to a new home helped him save Alex's life. "I guess we all owe Cat a bit of credit as well."

Savannah snapped a photo of him holding the cat. "You mean Mr. Meowgy?"

Jerry held his tongue. He didn't care one way or the other – it was enough that the cat had a home where he would be well loved. "If you say so."

Chapter Two

Traffic had just begun to thin out on Interstate 75 when the Durango's Uconnect alerted him of Seltzer's call. Jerry pushed the button on the steering wheel to connect. "Hey, Sergeant, what's up?"

"The blood pressure of the Captain of the Louisville Police Department. Apparently, the man arranged a press conference where he was going to introduce you and the dog, only neither of you showed up. He just called to ask me if I could locate you two." There was humor in Seltzer's voice.

Locating Jerry was easy; Gunter not so much. He hadn't seen his ghostly K-9 since leaving Louisville. Jerry wasn't worried; the dog often disappeared for short periods only to reappear – wagging his tail as if he'd been there all along. "What'd you tell him?"

"I told him you had a family emergency."

"More like a family disaster." Jerry groaned.

"How's that?"

"I'm heading to a family reunion."

"I thought you told me you weren't going."

"I wasn't, but my granny seems to think I

should."

Seltzer was quiet for a moment, and Jerry knew he was reaching for chewing gum. He'd traded one addiction for the other after quitting smoking ten years prior. "Would that be the same granny whose funeral you went to about five years ago?"

"It would."

"Boy, I wish I had your talent. There are some people I'd love to talk with again."

"Trust me, it's not half as cool as it sounds." Jerry rolled his neck. While some sprits were enjoyable to speak with, there were just as many who had left the world with a chip on their shoulder.

"No, I guess it's not. My luck, I'd get a visit from my mother-in-law. The woman hated me. I'm sure she hasn't mellowed since her demise. Still, if you hear from Hoffa, ask him where his body is. That'd be a feather in my cap if I uncovered that mystery."

Jerry laughed. "I'll be sure to ask if he ever shows up."

"Have you told your folks you quit the force yet?"

"Nope."

"I'll cover for you if you'd like." That was the thing about his old boss – the man always had his back.

"Thanks, but they're going to find out sooner or later. I may as well get it over with."

"Let me know if you change your mind."

"Will do."

"And, McNeal?"

"Yeah, Seltzer?"

"Try to have some fun."

Jerry chuckled. "It's easy to tell you've never met my family."

"Yes, well, try anyway."

"Will do."

"Okay, son, I've got to go. Call if you need anything."

"Will do." Seltzer's number disappeared from the dash monitor, and Jerry drummed his fingers on the wheel. Best to get the call over with. He pressed the button, bringing the monitor to life once more. "Call Mom."

A second later, his mother's voice rang out. "Hello, Jerry, are you okay?"

Jerry sighed. It was the same way she'd answered each and every call of his since his brother died. "Yeah, Mom. I'm fine."

"Oh, good. It sounds like you're driving? You know it's not safe to drive and hold the phone. I worry about you driving around in the old truck your grandmother left you. Unless you're in your police car, then I guess it's okay. I see police in Florida talking on the phone all the time. Are you still there? You're awfully quiet, Jerry."

Just waiting for you to take a breath. "I'm here, Mom. Don't worry, I'm using hands-free."

"So you are working." The disappointment was evident in her voice. "I'd hoped you'd be able to come to the reunion this year. You've missed so many."

"That's what I called to tell you, Mom. I'll be there." He thought about telling her that Granny had insisted upon it, but he wasn't sure if his dad was listening. While his mother understood his gift, his father was less enthusiastic.

"You're coming?" The transformation in her voice made Jerry smile. "Oh, Jerry, that is wonderful. Everyone will be so happy to see you. I'll let Marvin know so he can get you a room ready."

"Save it for someone else. I already have a place to stay."

"There's no need to pay for a hotel. Uncle Marvin has plenty of room in his cabin."

"I'm not paying for a room. I'm staying at a friend's cabin." He decided against telling her it was twenty miles away.

"A friend? What friend? Someone from school?"

"No, Mom, friends from Louisville. They have a cabin nearby and are letting me use it while I'm here."

"That's nice of them. But I'm sure Uncle Marvin would…"

"Mom, I'm good. Besides, I'm used to living on my own and I'll be a lot more comfortable there."

Far away from Marvin.

"You have to stop blaming Uncle Marvin for Joseph's death. He was just as upset as everyone else. He even sued the business owner."

Jerry started to tell her that her uncle sued anyone that looked at him the wrong way but decided against it. When it came to Marvin, everyone in the family wore blinders. "Mom, I don't want to stay at Uncle Marvin's and that's final."

"Okay, son, whatever you say. Where are you? You remembered to bring an extra jug of water for the radiator, didn't you? Your grandma always had a devil of a time keeping that truck cool."

"I fixed the radiator a long time ago, but I don't have the truck anymore. I bought something new."

"You sold it?"

"Nope. I gave it away."

"Gave it away?"

"More like donated it to the cars for veterans program."

"That was nice of you. Granny would have liked that."

"I believe so too. Listen, the service is getting fuzzy." It was a lie – there was nothing wrong with the phone service. Jerry swallowed his guilt. "I'm going to go. I'll see you in a couple of hours."

"Okay, Jerry. Drive safe."

"I will." Jerry disconnected the call and ran a hand over the back of his neck. As he did, Gunter appeared in the passenger seat. He looked over at the dog. "This is going to be a fun weekend."

Gunter yawned and Jerry laughed. "Don't worry, dog, it will be anything but boring."

***

As Jerry drove through his hometown of Newport, Tennessee, his mind was filled with memories from his childhood – including those which involved his younger brother, Joseph. Though Jerry was only a year older, Joseph had worshiped him. Jerry couldn't go anywhere without Joseph tagging along. The two were so much alike in both looks and body composition that people often thought they were twins, something the boys rarely corrected. Jerry didn't mind Joey's adoration unless there were girls involved, then Jerry preferred to have a little space. That need for privacy had cost them both dearly.

Jerry stopped in front of his childhood home on Green Acres Drive. He stared at the brick house, remembering the event that had changed the course of their lives. Weeks into the start of school, Jerry had finally gathered the courage to talk to a new girl that had joined his class. It took him all morning to summon up his courage, only to have her walk away without responding. The rest of the day hadn't gone any better, and he'd insisted Joseph leave him alone and go hang out with his own friends. His radar had pinged, but Jerry thought he was picking up on his

18

brother's hurt feelings.

Dealing with humiliation and heartbreak of his own, he had ignored the warning. Jerry let off the brake, his mind still on the past as he pulled away from the curb.

Joseph and his friends had followed the train tracks through town and beyond – spray-painting graffiti along the route. What could have been labeled childish stupidity turned into a federal offense when the group decided to leave their marks on government property, something that couldn't be denied as each boy had foolishly signed their handiwork with their initials. A federal record meant no government jobs and kept Joseph from following Jerry into the Marine Corps. At the time, Jerry was relieved his brother wouldn't be following him into battle and told a devastated Joseph it would keep him safe. "What a crock of shit."

Gunter whined a squeaky yawn.

Realizing he'd spoken out loud, Jerry rolled his neck and flexed his fingers, which were white from gripping the wheel. "Better get used to it, dog. Going home always brings out the crazy in me."

If only I hadn't pushed him away that day. Jerry pressed on the gas, gripping the steering wheel once more. To add to his guilt, he'd discovered the girl in question – one Patricia Jean O'Conner – wasn't being rude. Jerry had caught her totally off guard and she'd run away to gather her thoughts. The next day,

Patricia stuck a note inside his locker telling him she liked him too. The young romance was short-lived as Patricia's mother was worried about not only the girl's grades but her virtue, and took it upon herself to home school her only daughter. But for an entire school year, Patti – the cutest little redhead in town – was his girl.

He drove across town to North Street, driving slow past Patti's childhood home, hoping to get a glimpse of something that would tell him her parents still lived there and could tell him of her whereabouts. *Give it a rest, Jerry; it's been over fifteen years.* What was it about a person's first love? Maybe the simple innocence of it all. Then again, his first true love had appeared when he was fifteen, and his thoughts had been anything but pure.

Jerry smiled, remembering the massive amount of freckles that covered her skin. More than once, he'd fantasized about using his fingers to connect all the dots – promising himself he would not leave one spot untouched. The only thing that had stopped him was that she had three older brothers. "I can take them."

Jerry glanced in the rearview mirror, surprised to see he was blushing. Patti Cakes; he hadn't thought about her in years. *I wonder if she's married. Maybe I should look her up while I'm in town. I haven't changed all that much since high school.* Jerry ran a hand through his hair, which was slightly longer than buzz length since he'd stopped shaving his skull a few weeks ago. He let the hand slide over the stubble on his face and glanced in the mirror, trying to decide if he looked rugged or homeless. *Best go for homeless since you live in your car.* Jerry heaved a sigh. If anyone would be connecting the dots, it would be Patti. Even if he were to get lucky enough to find her still single, she'd send him packing the moment she discovered him to be without a job or roof over his head. "Quit being so hard on yourself, Jerry. You have a lot to offer. You're far from broke, you drive a really hot ride, and you have a dog that you never need to feed or clean up after."

Jerry looked over at Gunter and laughed when the dog smiled a K-9 smile and wagged his tail. He ruffled the dog's fur. "We're so fine, we should be on the cover of *GQ* magazine."

Gunter barked his approval and Jerry howled in return.

The hair on Jerry's arms tingled and he looked in the rear mirror to see his grandmother sitting in the back seat. Though he'd felt her presence recently, this was the first time he'd actually seen her since speaking to her at her funeral.

She smiled when he noticed her.

"Good to see you, Granny." He held his breath, waiting to see if he would be able to hear her response.

"It's about time you came home."

Jerry's heartbeat increased. "I can both see and hear you."

"Back seat, dog." In an instant, she and Gunter traded places. "I told you I'd be here."

"Why couldn't I see you this morning?"

"I didn't want you to."

"Why not?"

She shrugged. "Incentive. If I had shown myself, you might not have come."

That's true.

"Of course it's true. I know you better than you know yourself."

"I see you can still read my mind."

"Yes."

Jerry remembered his earlier thoughts about Patti and blushed. His grandmother frowned and looked out the window.

"I didn't know you were near."

She turned to face him and her smile returned. "I'm always near you." She laughed. "I give you privacy when it is warranted."

"I was just kidding about connecting the dots."

She placed her hand on his and he felt a sudden sorrow. "No you weren't, but that doesn't matter now."

"Why not?"

"We can talk later. I need to go."

Jerry started to object but it was too late – she was gone.

Chapter Three

Jerry drove past the entrance to his uncle's driveway three times before finally turning and taking the snaking path that led to Marvin's cabin. He parked in the driveway next to his parents' Chrysler and surveyed the landscape. Jerry would have found the four-story cabin with wraparound porches on each level rather magnificent if not for the fact that he knew it had been purchased with blood money. Funds awarded when Marvin sued the owner of the property and the builders who oversaw the pouring of the driveway that collapsed, sending Marvin's tree-trimming truck toppling over the hillside. Joseph had been harnessed into the truck's lift bucket at the time, trimming branches from trees close to the house, and was pronounced dead at the scene – he was twenty-one years old.

No stranger to the art of litigation, Marvin had successfully sued both the property owner and construction company on his great-nephew's behalf. Jerry was stunned to learn that Joseph's will had listed him as his beneficiary. By the time the dust settled with Joseph's life insurance, company insurance payouts, and wrongful death settlements, Jerry had well over two million dollars in the bank. Money he hadn't touched until recently when Joseph's ghost had declared Jerry a cheapskate and urged him to spend some of the money on a new ride.

Jerry drummed his fingers on the steering wheel. "What am I doing here?"

Gunter growled when Jerry stretched his index finger toward the push-button start.

Jerry sighed. "You too, Gunter?"

Gunter gave a small yip in return.

"Fine, have it your way, but you'd better keep an eye on me. I can't promise not to throw Uncle Marvin off the fourth-floor balcony."

Gunter tilted his head in disapproval.

"I know the man's old, but spend a few minutes with him and tell me you don't feel the same way." Jerry opened the door and got out. He pushed down the lock, not wanting to alert those inside to his arrival by honking the remote. Gunter glued himself to Jerry's left leg as Jerry started toward the house. The door opened and several small children piled out. Oblivious to his presence, they headed off to a large play structure in the backyard. They were followed outside by a full-size black lab, who took one look in Jerry's direction and alerted with a deep, throaty growl. Gunter answered with one of his own, and Jerry lowered his hand to silence his ghostly companion. The lab whimpered then took off after the children with his tail tucked between his legs.

Jerry looked at Gunter. "I hope you are pleased with yourself."

Gunter growled and wagged his tail.

"Listen, dude, you're welcome to come along, but don't go starting any more trouble."

"Are you coming in, or are you going to stand there talking to yourself all day?"

Jerry looked to the second-floor balcony and saw his dad standing there with a beer in his hand. *Great, as if the man doesn't already think you're crazy.* "The kids are outside. I was checking for bears."

"They're alright as long as they've got the dog with them. Sammy's not scared of anything."

Except ghost dogs.

Gunter stayed at Jerry's side as he made his way inside the cabin. The ground floor was set up for entertainment with a pool table, foosball and air hockey tables, and several arcade-level video game machines. On the other side of the room sat a wraparound couch and a huge pile of bean bag chairs facing a 72-inch TV. The living space also had a full kitchen with a wet bar complete with a full-size coke machine and movie theater popcorn maker.

Jerry bypassed the elevator, opting to take the stairs to the main living area. While the walkout basement was the ultimate play area, this level was set up more for adult living. A custom leather couch and several recliners sat in the open concept great room, which shared the floor with a designer kitchen. The walls were knotty pine, and massive windows showcased breathtaking mountain views.

The elevator dinged. The door opened and Marvin stepped out of the box. He'd aged in the years since Jerry had last seen him, but the gut-punch of seeing the man was the same as always. Marvin's brows knitted upon seeing him. Jerry drew his pistol and pulled the trigger, emptying his magazine into the man.

Jerry felt the weight of Gunter's body leaning against his leg. His vision cleared and he watched as Marvin limped closer. Jerry had envisioned the same scenario for as long as he could remember. Marvin was a war hero in Vietnam who had received three Purple Hearts and the Congressional Medal of Honor. Surely he could survive being shot multiple times at point-blank range – that is, if he were the man he claimed to be. The trouble was, his uncle hadn't been in Vietnam or any other war. Uncle Marvin had been in an accident when he was young that left one leg two inches shorter than the other, making him ineligible to enlist. But every year during the Cobb family reunion, Marvin revisited all the things that had happened to him during the war. All the people he'd saved, enemies he'd killed. The worst part was that no one called him on it. Ever.

When Jerry would ask, the family would make

excuses. He'd had a tough life. His eggs were scrambled in the accident.

That was a lie. His body might have been mangled a bit, but his brain worked perfectly. Marvin could remember every story he'd ever read or heard and made his own. Most of the time, Jerry could distance himself and ignore the man, but that changed at the gathering after Joseph's funeral when Marvin relived his time in the Afghanistan war and how he nearly got his leg blown off. The man even had the gall to pull up his pants leg to show the scars.

What burned Jerry most was that Marvin was not in the Afghanistan War. Jerry was. Only Jerry didn't like to talk about it. It was that way with most who were there. When you see the things he saw over there, see your "brothers" get blown up right in front of you, well, you just don't talk about that. You compartmentalize it and move the hell on.

Marvin's stories were hard to swallow to begin with, but when his uncle started talking about people Jerry actually knew – Marines he'd served with, men he'd heard scream in pain while trying his best to patch them up until the medic arrived, only to have them die in his arms. Good men who deserved better than to be looped in his great uncle's fantasy existence; that was something that made Jerry want to put a bullet in the man.

"Jerry, my boy. Good to see you!"

Jerry struggled to be polite. "Hello, Uncle. Some

place you have here."

Marvin smiled and waved him in. "Come on in. Stella's in town with your mom. She'll find you a room when she gets back."

Stella was Marvin's second wife and twenty-some years his junior. She wore her age well, with the exception of her preference of dressing like a Kardashian. Jerry shook his head. "No need to bother. I'm not staying."

Marvin frowned. "You're not coming to the reunion?"

"I'll be here tomorrow. I'm staying at a friend's cabin just a few miles away."

"Don't be ridiculous. We have plenty of room."

"I prefer my privacy."

"Yes, the war will do that to a man. Why, I remember when I came home…"

Easy, Jerry, stay calm. "Dad's out on the deck. I'm going to go say hello."

Marvin nodded to the fridge. "There's beer in the icebox."

Jerry crossed to the fridge, pulled out a can of Bud, and stepped out on the deck. Gunter walked to the middle and stretched out in the sun.

His father, Wayne, leaned against the railing, watching the kids play. "You see Marvin?"

Jerry joined him by the rail and slid a glance at his father, noting he'd lost weight he didn't have to lose. "I did."

"I didn't hear gunshots, so I guess it's safe to assume you didn't shoot him."

Jerry pulled the tab on the can and took a drink. "I thought about it."

His father chuckled. "I commend you for not following through."

Something was up – his father was being too civil. The man had had a chip on his shoulder when it came to Jerry ever since the incident with Joseph and the spray paint. "You feeling okay, Pop? You seem a bit more mellow than I remember."

"Don't be reading anything into it. I'm tired. It was a long drive in yesterday and Marvin had me up late telling me stories."

Jerry took another gulp of beer. "I'll not be listening to any of those."

"From the way he looks, Marvin won't be around to tell them much longer."

Jerry had thought the same thing. "Not my problem."

"No. I don't suppose it is. You never have had much time for family."

And there it was. Jerry rubbed his hand across the top of his head and took a sip of beer.

"What's with the hair? Don't tell me the state boys have relaxed their standards."

Jerry had thought he would at least be able to finish his beer before they got into it. *Best get it over with*. "I'm not a state trooper anymore."

His dad crumpled the can in his hand. "You got fired?"

"No. I quit."

"Sounds about right."

Jerry couldn't blame the man for being upset, but the disappointment in his father's voice hurt all the same. Jerry pushed away from the railing.

"That's it; run away without a word."

Jerry whirled on him. "What do you expect me to say? That you're right? I've never lived up to your expectations in the past. Why should I start now?"

"That's a load of horse crap and you know it."

Gunter rose to his haunches, intently watching both men. Jerry raised his hand to steady the K-9 before answering. "The hell it is. You've been angry with me ever since Joseph got in trouble for the graffiti."

"I was disappointed in both of you at the time, but I got over that years ago. You were Joseph's brother, not his keeper."

Jerry ran his hand over his head. "You never treated me the same."

"That's because you never acted the same. You took Joseph's punishment harder than he did. You let the guilt from that one foolish decision dictate your whole life. Hell, the only reason you joined the Marines was so you could run away from your guilt."

Truth. Jerry ran his hand through his hair once

more. "When Joseph died, you said…"

"I've said a lot of things I regret over the years. But I was trying to get you to fight back. I thought if I pushed you hard enough, you'd get mad and let all that anger out."

"I'm not mad at you."

"No. You're angry at yourself. You have seventeen years' worth of could've-would've-should-haves gnawing at you, and you won't let anyone in. You want me to say I'm sorry? Okay, I'm sorry! There, I said it. But it's not me that you need to hear it from. You need to forgive yourself. You have a – what is it you call it? A feeling? Your grandmother used to call it a gift. Some gift if it doesn't allow you to be human. You are, you know? And I'm sorry to tell you this, but we humans make mistakes. It's just that most of us don't let a small mistake dictate our whole lives."

Jerry worked to keep his emotions in check. "That small mistake got Joseph killed. If not for that, he would have enlisted in the Marines."

"Where he would have probably died in the war."

Jerry closed his eyes to ward off the image.

"It was his time to go. You couldn't have saved him any more than if you'd been here and told him not to get in the truck." His father's lips were trembling. "I didn't push you away, Jerry. You left and I didn't know how to get you back. I'm tired of dancing around our feelings. I promised your grandmother if she'd get you to come to the reunion, I would try to make things right."

Jerry blinked his surprise. "You're telling me you talked to Granny?"

"No, not in the way you do. But I've prayed for her to hear me a few times over the last couple of months. I went and sat beside her grave yesterday." He looked up and Jerry saw tears brimming his eyes. "I begged her to help me get my boy back before it's too late."

Jerry blew out a long breath of air and felt as though an invisible weight had been lifted off his shoulders. "What are we supposed to do now, Pop?"

Wayne wiped the tears from his eyes. "The devil if I know."

Chills ran the length of Jerry's spine as Gunter lifted his head and howled. From out in the yard, the lab joined in, much to the delight of the children who ran toward the dog, mimicking his howl.

Jerry's father looked over the railing. "What in tarnation has gotten into them?"

Jerry remained silent. He'd just gotten his dad back; he didn't want to take a chance at pushing him away again.

Chapter Four

Jerry heard a car door and walked to the far side of the deck. A minivan had pulled in next to his parents' car. "Looks like the ladies are home. I should go see if they need help."

"They'll be fine. Marie and Robert are with them."

Marie and Robert were Stella's daughter and son-in-law who shared the house and helped look after the place. "How many kids do they have now?"

"Four or five – enough to sound like a herd of horses when you're trying to sleep."

Jerry laughed. "Glad I'm not spending the night."

Wayne raised an eyebrow. "Your mom said you weren't. Marvin has plenty of room, you know."

"I prefer my privacy. Besides, I promised my friends I would look in on their place for them." He added the last part to keep from getting pushback from his father. Jerry saw his mom staring in his direction and waved. She smiled and returned the gesture. "How's Florida?"

"Hot and full of gnats."

Jerry turned in his direction. "Mom said you like it there. Was she wrong?"

"I love it. But that's beside the point; you asked how it is. You should visit sometime. Your mom will let you drive her golf cart."

Jerry laughed. "I'll pass."

"Told you about it, did she?"

"I saw pictures of it on Facebook. The pink suits her, but I can't see you driving it." Actually, Jerry had spent more time than he cared to admit to stalking his parents' Facebook page. From the looks of the pictures the two posted, it seemed as though they were having the time of their lives since moving to The Villages, Florida.

Wayne moved away from the railing and sat in one of the Adirondack chairs spread around the deck. "I don't need to drive it. I'm a man of leisure now that I retired. Imagine that. Your mother went all her life refusing to get her driver's license and now she drives me anywhere I want to go. They have paths for the golf carts and map apps you can download to your phone, so she doesn't get lost."

"It sounds like the two of you are living your best life."

Wayne waved his hand. "Almost. There are plenty of sourpusses that live there, but your mom's become rather adept at saluting."

"Saluting?"

"She climbs inside that little pink cart with her

nails painted to match and something comes over her. Someone cuts her off or blows their horn and…" His father extended his middle finger. "You should be proud. The woman's a natural."

Jerry laughed at the image. "She even drives you to the golf course?"

"Most days. Your mom has a golf bag to match her cart and her clubs have pink handles. She can't hit the ball very far, but it goes straight as an arrow. Oh, and I'm not supposed to know this, but Lori ordered me a custom cart for my birthday." His father looked over his shoulder, then smiled. "It looks just like a '57 Chevy. Don't say anything unless she tells you – she forgot and left the invoice on the counter and doesn't know I saw it."

Way to go, Mom. His father had talked about buying a '57 Chevy for as long as Jerry could remember. "I have to admit I was worried when you guys said you were selling everything and moving to Florida. I'm glad to hear it's everything you thought it would be."

"It's a good fit for us. Your mom doesn't like to cook all that much anymore, and I never got around to learning. There are enough restaurants in the area that we don't get bored. We have friends there and enjoy all the activities they have for us old geezers. Heck, if it wasn't for driving up here, we wouldn't even need a car."

Jerry wanted to be happy for his parents, but his

father's words drove home the point that he himself no longer had a place he could call home. At least while his parents still maintained a residence in Newport, he could think about going home. Since resigning his position with the Pennsylvania State Police, all his earthly belongings were in the backseat of his Durango and his mailing address was a P.O. box that Seltzer checked once a week. *Stop with the pity party, Jerry. Your current state of being is of your own design.* Jerry managed a smile. "That's good, Pop. It really is."

The door opened – Marvin hobbled out, looking slightly disheveled. "I fell asleep in the recliner. I guess it's better than falling asleep on watch and letting my guys down."

Gunter gave a warning yip as if to remind him to behave. Jerry ran his hand over the top of his head to calm himself.

Marvin walked to the far end of the deck and looked toward the driveway. "That your ride out there, Jer?"

"Yep."

"Looks pretty sharp. What is it? A V-8?"

"Yep, a hemi."

"'Bout time you bought you something new. I don't know why Betty Lou thought to leave you with that old clunker of hers."

"I guess she thought it fit me at the time."

"Naw, that ain't the truth of it. The truth of it was

she didn't have anyone else to pawn it off on and knew you were too polite to tell her no. Why, I remember…"

Jerry took that as his cue to leave. "I'm going to go say hi to Mom."

"Good job keeping the peace," Wayne whispered as he walked past.

Stella was in the kitchen emptying the bags of groceries that littered the counter. Trim as ever and rather well-endowed for her petite size, she currently wore shorts short enough to make a woman half her age blush. When Marvin had first announced his plans to marry the woman, Jerry had thought she was nothing but a gold digger. Even his grandmother had expressed concern over their difference in age. From everything Jerry had seen and heard, the woman – who came into the marriage with three children – seemed to care deeply about Marvin – who'd lost his wife two years prior to their meeting. Stella had just come out of a turbulent marriage and Marvin was happy to pick up the pieces. While Marvin was a pain in the ass, Jerry had never heard him raise his voice to anyone and appeared to worship his new bride. Still, Jerry often wondered if Stella was in denial of her husband's eccentricities or if she was just as crazy as the man she'd married. She squealed and threw her arms around Jerry's neck. "Jerry, it's so good to see you again. Did you talk to Marvin? I know he's going to be thrilled to have someone he can trade war stories with."

The elevator dinged, the door slid open, and Robert and Marie, both of whom carried armloads of groceries, stepped out.

Jerry gave them a pleading look before answering, "I saw him briefly. We haven't had time to catch up just yet. I was just going to find Mom."

Marie – a younger, more conservative version of her mother – smiled as she hefted the load she was carrying onto the counter. "Mother, Jerry's turning blue. Turn him loose before you suffocate him."

"I can't help it. Jerry here is so handsome. I just know this is what my Marvie looked like when he was younger. Oh, what I wouldn't give to be able to go back in time and get some of that." Stella released him and looked him up and down.

Jerry shuddered. He didn't know which was worse: being compared to his uncle or knowing the unspoken thought that had just passed through Stella's mind.

"Isn't that sweet? He's blushing. Don't get yourself all worked up, darling. I'm as faithful as a love-sick puppy. I'm just playing with you." Stella winked, then turned her attention back to the grocery bag she'd been emptying.

Robert gave him a better-you-than-me smirk and nodded toward the elevator. "Lori's still downstairs. She did a little shopping and wanted to put her stuff in her car before coming up."

Jerry opted for the stairs – taking them two at a time with Gunter following. His mother was just transferring the last bag when he joined her. Other than her hair, which was clipped into a short, flattering cut, and a tan that showcased her yoga-toned body, his mother hadn't changed a bit since he'd last seen her.

She slammed the trunk and bit her bottom lip. "Your face is flushed. I take it you had an encounter with Stella."

"I'm pretty sure I need a shower." Jerry moved and looked in the side wing mirror of the car. "She thinks I look like Marvin. I don't see it."

"She's right. You've always resembled my side of the family." His mother stretched out her arms and waved him forward with slender fingers. "You going to give your mother a hug, or are you saving them all for Stella?"

Jerry noted the pink nails and smiled, picturing her flashing the bird at those who taunted her. He walked into her embrace, closing his eyes when she wrapped her arms around him. "It's good to see you, Mom."

"It's good to see you, Jerry." She released him, cocking her head as if trying to figure something out. "You seem…different."

Jerry ran his hand over his scalp. "Probably because it's the first time in twelve years you've seen me with hair."

"Perhaps. But I think there's more to it." Her eyes widened. "Wayne talked to you, didn't he?"

Jerry smiled. "We had a nice chat."

"He said he was going to. I just didn't know he would get to it so soon. So everything is good with you two?"

"Let's just say everything is different."

Lori frowned. "Good different?"

Jerry sighed. "Yeah, Mom."

The worry lines lessened. "Oh, thank God. I've been so worried about him."

"Dad's lost weight. Is there something going on?" Jerry had been trying to get a reading on the man but hadn't picked up anything that concerned him.

"Nothing scary, if that's what you mean."

"But there is something."

Lori turned and placed her backside against the trunk of her car, and Jerry joined her, watching as Gunter walked through the yard sniffing the ground.

Oblivious to the dog's presence, his mother continued. "I like your new ride."

"Thanks."

"I knew moving to Florida would be different but didn't realize how much things would change."

Jerry kicked at the gravel with the toe of his boot. "Dad made it sound as if you guys like the place."

"Oh, we do. Leaving here was the best decision we ever made."

"I thought you were happy here."

"We love Newport. And I do miss the mountains and some of my friends. There were just too many memories tying us to the place. And, as you know, not all of them were good. Maybe there is something in the water in The Villages or maybe it's just because we don't have a constant reminder of what happened to Joseph, but your father has mellowed."

"I can see that."

"Did he tell you he's seeing a therapist?"

That explains a lot. "No."

"Well, he has. The guilt of his actions has been weighing on him. Thus the weight loss. He hears his friends talking about their kids, and he sits there with nothing to add. He'd made up his mind that if you didn't show up this weekend, we were driving to Pennsylvania to see you."

"That would've been a wasted trip."

"Because you're unable to forgive him?"

"Because I don't live there anymore. I quit the force."

Lori gasped. "Quit? Where do you live?"

Jerry resisted pointing at his Durango. "I'm still trying to figure that out."

"We have an extra room."

Jerry chuckled. "Thanks, but I'm a bit too old to be living with my parents."

His mother blew out a sigh. "That's good. Our community has rules about that."

Jerry lifted her hand and kissed the back of it. "And yet you offered anyway."

"Of course, you're our son."

Jerry released her hand. "You know, Mom, all of this touchy-feely stuff from you and Dad might take a bit of getting used to."

Lori grasped his hand. "That's okay; we've got time. You know, you can't hide out here all day."

"Is that what I'm doing?"

"Isn't it?"

"Yes. I just hoped it wasn't that obvious."

Chapter Five

The rest of the afternoon was a welcome surprise, as Jerry found he enjoyed his time catching up with the family. Even Marvin's stories took a tolerable direction after trying unsuccessfully multiple times to regale everyone with tales of his wartime escapades. Each time he started with one of his fictitious stories, Wayne or Lori would steer the conversation in a new direction. After the fourth such event, Jerry realized that both his mother and father were running block to keep him from leaving early. The only one who didn't seem to be enjoying himself was Sammy – the poor dog had been on edge since their arrival. Jerry decided to take his leave and give the dog a chance to relax. The moment he stood, Gunter jumped up, eager to see where he was going.

Sammy growled. Robert shushed the lab and shrugged his apology. "I don't know what's gotten into that crazy mutt. He's been acting spooked all afternoon."

Marie frowned. "Maybe there's a bear in the area."

Jerry had his money on spooked – if there were

a bear in the area, Gunter would have picked up on it as well. The truth of the matter was dogs – normal dogs – didn't like him. They never had. Add to that the fact that Sammy hadn't taken his eyes off Gunter since returning to the deck, and Jerry figured the lab was in danger of having a nervous breakdown. *Do dogs have panic attacks?* If they did, the poor fellow was dangerously close to having one. "Don't be too hard on Sammy. It's probably me – dogs have never liked me."

Marvin peered in Gunter's direction, and for a moment, Jerry thought the man ready to give away his secret. *He knows Gunter's here. Don't be silly, Jerry. He probably just thought of another story to tell.* Either way, the man's reaction bothered him. Jerry arched his back and stretched his arms over his head, drawing Marvin's attention away from Gunter. "I'm going to be heading out for the night."

His mother sighed. "So soon."

Jerry closed his eyes briefly. "I have a stop to make on the way out."

Lori nodded her understanding. "Tell Joseph we said hello."

Jerry walked to where his mother sat and kissed her on the top of her head. He smiled at everyone sitting around the deck – including Marvin – then made eye contact with his dad. "See you tomorrow."

Jerry walked down the stairs feeling as if he were being followed. He surveyed his surroundings and caught a glimpse of a shadow out of the corner of his right eye. Not Gunter, as the dog was plastered to his left leg. Jerry opened the driver's door, watching as Gunter leapt into the seat with a single bound. The dog hesitated then moved to the passenger seat. Jerry looked in the back and saw the reason for Gunter's hesitation. The shadow now filled the second-row seat.

Jerry felt a chill travel the length of his arms and looked at Gunter to gauge the dog's reaction. While the K-9's ears were twitching, he didn't seem upset. Jerry took that as a sign that the spirit following them didn't wish them harm. Jerry directed his attention to Gunter. "Seems as though we've picked up a hitchhiker."

Gunter growled a warning, and Jerry looked to see his father watching him from the upper deck. Jerry waved, got into the truck, shut the door, and fastened his seatbelt in one smooth motion. His dad was still watching as Jerry started the Durango and shifted into reverse. Jerry wheeled the SUV around, feeling the rumble from the hemi engine as he sped out of the driveway.

He stopped at the end of the long driveway and beat his head against the headrest. *Damn.* Why couldn't he be normal just for one day? Instead, he'd just reminded his father the man had a nut job for a son. Maybe he should forget the cabin and just keep driving. At least the memories he'd have from today's visit would be good ones.

Easy, Jerry, it isn't like this is the first time your father caught you talking to a ghost. He knows you're different. He said he wants to change. The least you can do is give him the benefit of the doubt. Jerry pushed the button to bring the Uconnect to life then thumbed until he found Doc's number.

"You good, McNeal?" As soon as he heard Doc's voice, Jerry's urge to run dissipated.

"Hey, Doc, just checking in. I wasn't in such a good place the last time I called, and I wanted to let you know I'm doing better." *At least until a few seconds ago.*

"Still in Kentucky?"

"No, I decided to head to Tennessee to see my folks. The downside is my uncle is here."

"That the guy with the war stories?"

"That's the one."

"You're not planning on shooting him, are you?"

"Does visualizing count?"

Laughter floated through the speakers. "If it turns into anything else, hit me up. I'll testify in your defense."

"Gonna tell them I'm crazy?"

More laughter. "Aren't we all?"

"I reckon we are."

"Christ, McNeal, been in the south less than a month, and you're already getting your twang back."

Jerry chuckled. "This ain't nothin'. The longer I

stay, the slower I'll talk. Listen, I don't want to keep you. I just needed to hear your voice." It was the truth, but that didn't make admitting it less weird.

"You still seeing that ghost?"

Even though Jerry knew Doc was talking about his ghostly K-9 companion, he glanced in the rearview mirror, taking in the image of the shadow. "Yep."

"You good, McNeal?"

The hell if I know. No use admitting it as there wasn't anything the man could do to help with his current situation. "Golden, Doc."

"You need an ear, you know where to find me."

"Works both ways, you know."

Doc was quiet for so long, Jerry thought he'd dropped the call.

"I may just take you up on that one day."

Something in Doc's voice worried him. "You good, Doc?"

"Don't go reading anything into that, McNeal. If I need you, I'll call."

Jerry wanted to press for more, but it was too late – the dash display lit up, showing the call had ended. Jerry made a mental note to check in with the man soon.

***

The shadowed presence stayed with them all the way to Mineral Street, leaving when Jerry turned into Union Cemetery. The tension in Jerry's shoulders eased as he drove past the stones and found his was the only vehicle in sight. He parked off to the side at the end of the row and sat without exiting for several moments. He saw movement out of the corner of his eye, thought maybe the shadow had returned, and breathed a sigh of relief when he saw Gunter sitting outside the Durango waiting for him. Jerry shut off the engine and opened the door. "You're turning into a real nag, you know."

Gunter lowered into a bow and growled.

Jerry laughed. "You don't want to be called a nag, then stop nagging."

Gunter barked, turning in circles as he wagged his tail. For a moment, it reminded him of the old *Lassie* reruns he used to watch with his granny. When the collie had acted in such a manner, it usually meant something was wrong, and the dog wanted Timmy to follow. He doubted that was the case, but he followed just to be sure. "I'm coming, already. I don't know why you're so excited."

Gunter ignored him, running ahead then stopping and egging him forward with enthusiastic yips.

Unlike the dog, Jerry wasn't as eager to reach the stones that marked both his brother's and grandmother's graves. Gunter stood with his tail wagging, letting Jerry know they weren't alone. Unfazed by the knowledge, he stood reading the etching on the headstones.

Joseph Cody McNeal, Son, Brother, March

13,1991 – September 29, 2012

Next to Joseph's stone was the one belonging to his grandmother. He skimmed the lettering. Betty Lou Cobb, October 9,1938 – November 2, 2017

Though he'd seen his brother's grave numerous times over the years, it was the first time he'd seen his grandmother's headstone, as he hadn't returned since the day he watched them place her casket in the freshly dug earth. Jerry blew out a ragged breath. "I miss you, Granny."

"What am I? Chopped liver?"

Jerry smiled. "Joseph?"

"Boo."

"Very funny." Jerry turned and disappointment raced through him. Even though he could feel his brother's presence and hear his voice, he could not see his brother's image.

"I wasn't trying to be funny. I was trying to scare you."

"I haven't been scared of ghosts since I was a kid." That was the thing. He'd seen spirits for as long as he could remember. So why couldn't he see his brother? It didn't make any sense. "Why can't I see you?"

"Because you don't want to."

"Don't be ridiculous. I'm here, ain't I?"

"You're the one being ridiculous. Tell me you can't see the old lady to your right. Or the little girl picking wildflowers. How about the man stooping to pull the weeds in front of his stone? Tell me you can't see him."

Joseph was right; he could see them all. Plus, he'd seen his grandmother earlier in the day. So it was just Joseph he couldn't see. No, that wasn't true. While he'd felt the spirit that left the cabin with him, he had not fully seen it. That wasn't his brother's spirit. At least he didn't think so. "That wasn't you that rode over here with me, was it?"

"Nope. I've been waiting for you – figured you'd show up sooner or later. Now if you want to see me, you'll have to want to."

"Of course, I want to."

"If you did, you would've seen me the moment you started down the row. Gunter saw me, didn't you, boy?"

Gunter tilted his head and gave a happy yip.

That explained the dog's eagerness for him to follow. Jerry ran his hand over his head.

"You're afraid to face me because of the guilt you feel."

"Jesus, you sound just like Dad."

"That's because it's the truth. None of this was your fault."

"What are you, a mind reader now?"

"Being a ghost has its advantages."

"Like?"

"Like being privy to private conversations. I heard you talking to Dad. It's about time the two of you got your shit together. You need to take what he said on board and stop blaming yourself for my death. Dad is right. It was my time. It didn't matter where I was; the outcome would have been the same."

Jerry sighed. "It sucks."

"Yep. It does. We were kids – kids do stupid things. What I never told you is I'd already made plans to go with them that day."

Jerry felt the punch as sure as if Joseph had hit him. He'd been carrying around the guilt of his brother's actions for the last seventeen years. "Then why didn't you ever say anything?!"

"Because I was a kid and you were willing to do anything for me after that. I was a regular pain in the ass, yet you never called me on it. I had a good thing going. I wasn't about to mess that up." Joseph shrugged. "Hello, big brother."

Jerry swallowed his emotions. It was like looking in the mirror, seeing himself from ten years ago. "It's good to see you, Joseph."

"And yet, your face shows you to be disappointed."

"Because I want so bad to be angry with you."

"But you can't because I'm dead." Joseph stuffed his hands into his pockets. "You got the shit end of the stick, Jerry. You took the blame then, and your anger continued to fester after my death. No wonder your head is so messed up."

"My head has nothing to do with this."

"Of course it does. Even Granny agrees."

"How come Granny's not here?"

"She doesn't like seeing her name on the headstone."

"Neither do I."

"It's just a stone. It's not like we're tied to this place."

That was true. He had often felt Joseph's presence. "How come you didn't say anything until now?"

"Granny told me not to. She said the healing couldn't take place without you hearing things from all parties. That's why she made me wait until Dad was ready."

"And if he'd never said anything?"

"Granny was working on him. He didn't tell you, but she haunted his dreams."

Jerry remembered the dreams he'd had just before leaving Pennsylvania. "Like you plagued mine?"

Joseph winked. "Let's just say it was an orchestrated effort."

"Why was it so important I come home?"

"You have things to take care of."

"I already talked to Dad."

"Other things."

"Like?"

Joseph bent and ruffled Gunter's fur. "How do

you like the dog?"

That Joseph hadn't answered was not lost on him. "He's cool."

"And that zombie makeup job I did?"

"That was you?"

"Most of it was the dog. But I put him up to it. Had a heck of a time getting him put back together."

Jerry ran his hand over his head. "What's it like? Being dead?"

"Nope. You don't get to ask that."

"Why not?"

"Every circumstance is different depending on the spirit. If you ask the wrong ghost, it could sway things. There's an unwritten rule. We don't say anything that would compromise life choices in either direction." Joseph dipped his hand into his pocket and pulled out a bright orange ball like the ones Jerry had bought for Gunter and never used. The moment the dog saw it, he sprang up, eager to give chase. "You really need to interact with him more, Jerry."

Before Jerry could answer, Joseph threw the ball to the other side of the lot. Jerry blinked his surprise. "I don't remember you having an arm like that."

"I've been practicing with Babe. You know, everyone knows him as a hitter. What most people don't know is he had a hell of a pitching arm."

Jerry blinked his surprise. "You're telling me you play ball with Babe Ruth...Babe Ruth the baseball player?"

Joseph winked and pulled his fingers across his mouth as if zipping his lips shut. "Hey, how come you never told me you could see ghosts? I mean, when we were kids."

Jerry Smiled a rueful smile. "I did, once. It was after Aunt Edna died. We were standing next to her coffin, and you made some comments about how it looked like she was sleeping. I told you she wasn't sleeping; she was standing right behind you. It scared you so bad, you stopped talking for a week."

"I don't remember that."

"It was a long time ago."

"Have you always been able to see ghosts?"

"I think so. For as long as I can remember anyway."

"Must have been cool."

Not really. "Some might think so."

"But not you?"

"Not at the time. But it's pretty cool getting to see and talk to you now."

Chapter Six

Hollow. That was the only way to explain the way Jerry felt. He'd spent over half his life blaming himself for something that wasn't his fault. How much time had he wasted while shrinks pried into his innermost thoughts trying unsuccessfully to whittle away at the guilt? Over what? A lie. If Joseph weren't already dead, he might just be inclined to strangle him. To further complicate things, what was he supposed to do with the information – just let it go and be normal? What the hell was normal anyway?

Jerry looked in the rear-view mirror at the shadowed spirit that had joined him the moment he drove out of the cemetery. *Not this. No, sir, this was bat shit crazy.*

He turned his frustration toward the spirit. "Who are you anyway? What do you want? And why the hell can't I see you?"

The entity remained voiceless.

Jerry looked to Gunter, whose otherworldly body filled the front passenger seat. "You got anything to say, dog?"

Gunter yawned.

Jerry ran his hand over his head. "How is this my life?"

***

The navigator alerted him of a turn. Jerry slowed then started the winding trek up the mountain to the cabin. At one point, the road doubled back on itself, the turn causing him to back up and reposition to continue the climb. Jerry momentarily regretted his decision to accept the invitation to use the cabin. *Relax, Jerry, you've watched too many horror films. It's not like you'll be alone in the woods.* He looked at Gunter. "You're not afraid of bears, are you?"

Gunter curled his lip and growled.

"Promise not to let one eat me?"

Another growl.

"Good to know."

The navigator announced his arrival and Jerry slowed, looking for the driveway. He came close to missing it before realizing the drive was nothing more than a dirt path shrouded with trees. Jerry made the turn, relaxing when the tree canopy opened, showing a picture-perfect log cabin – complete with a wraparound porch and mandatory swing – sitting on a relatively level lot.

Jerry parked, studied the small log structure, and looked in the mirror. "You're welcome to come inside, but I draw the line at sharing my bed."

The ghostly mist disappeared and reappeared on

the porch near the front door. For a moment, Jerry saw the shape of a woman and thought to take back the comment about sleeping alone. *Get a grip, Marine. You're not that desperate.*

The cabin before him was the direct opposite of the ostentatious cabin owned by his uncle. He much preferred this version, as it reminded him of a rustic standalone version of the apartment he'd rented in Pennsylvania. While he hadn't cared for his landlord, he'd enjoyed the coziness of the space.

Jerry opened the door, scanning the room. That was what he liked about small spaces, having the ability to detect threats with a single sweep. The kitchen, which sat to the right as he entered, proved basic but seemed to have all the necessary appliances, including a dishwasher. The main living room held a small bistro table with two chairs, a leather couch, matching recliner, and a coffee table. Jerry walked into the bedroom once again, surveying the room. Queen bed, dual bedside tables, a red heart-shaped Jacuzzi that took up an entire corner of the room. An image of Savannah and Alex flittered through his mind, and he shook it off. *At ease, Marine. Keep this up, and you'll be calling 1-800-OOh Babe before the night's over.*

The attached bathroom was surprisingly large with a decent-size walk-in subway-tiled shower. The shower seemed to be newly renovated, but that and the continued hardwood floors were where the niceties ended. Both the toilet and vanity top were jet black and extraordinarily small compared to their modern counterparts. Still, everything appeared to be clean and serviceable. He moved to the closet, verified it to be devoid of occupants, and closed the door once again. A second door hid a small shelf of tools and the hookups for a stackable washer and dryer. He closed the door, considered checking under the bed, then decided against it. He was near to the door when he hesitated. *Shit.* He returned to the bed, dropped to his knee, and looked underneath.

Jerry laughed at the absurdity. Here he was sharing the space with two ghosts, and he was worried about who might be hiding under the bed. He walked to the kitchen and lifted a note taped to the door of one of the cabinets.

Jerry, glad you made it safe. I live just down the road. Savannah called and asked me to stock the fridge and cabinets with a few things. Help yourself to whatever you like. I manage a few of the cabins in the area and am running to town several times a day. My card is in the drawer. I'm more than willing to pick up anything you might need. PS, Savannah asks that you give her a call when you get here, so she knows you made it safe. Meg.

Jerry opened the fridge and smiled when he saw two cases of beer, brats, lunchmeat, and several containers of preprepared deli salads. He pushed the Lite beer aside and pulled a Bud from the case. He pulled the tab, took a long drink, and set the can on the counter. Gunter followed as he returned to the Durango, pulled out his seabag and duffle bag, and took both inside, setting them near the bed. Ignoring the apparition that was literally following him around like a lost soul, he grabbed the beer, removed his Glock from his pants, and sank into the recliner. He took another drink then dialed Savannah's number, pleased to find he still had service.

"Jerry, did you find the place alright?"

"Found it just fine. As a matter of fact, I'm naked, sitting in your recliner and enjoying a beer."

Savannah laughed. "Ew."

"Not the response I was going for."

"I'm gay, remember?"

"Oh yeah, what was I thinking? In that case, I'm fully clothed, but I am drinking a beer."

"Sorry about the bathroom."

Jerry frowned. "What's wrong with the bathroom?"

"It's hideous. We're remodeling it in stages as we get extra money. We took out the tub and had the shower installed last year and are planning on hiring someone to redo the rest of it this summer."

"As long as the toilet flushes, it's fine in my book."

"Did you look under the bed?"

"Is that a guess, or are you reading me?"

"Neither. The woods give me the creeps, so I

always check all the closets and under the bed every time we arrive."

"Guilty."

"You're not scared to be there alone, are you?"

It was Jerry's time to laugh. "I think I can handle it. Besides, I'm not exactly alone."

"That's right, I forgot about your ghost buddy."

"Yeah, about that."

"Gunter's not with you?"

"Oh, he's with me, but I seem to have picked up a hitchhiker."

"That's dangerous."

"Not that kind of hitchhiker."

"I'm not following."

"She – at least I think it's a she – has been with me ever since I left my uncle's cabin."

"Do you know what she wants?"

"Not yet. But there was something I did find peculiar. I stopped by the cemetery to pay my respects and she didn't follow me. Yet when I left, she was with me again. Thoughts?"

"Maybe she doesn't acknowledge being dead. Like maybe she doesn't think she belongs in the cemetery."

"And yet, she thinks she's safe with me."

"Just make sure to either help her or take her with you when you leave. Alex is cool with you using the cabin, but she might not be as happy to find out we have a ghost squatting on the premises."

"You sure? It would make for a hell of a deterrent for burglars."

"That's one way to look at it. But seriously, Jerry, if this ghost has attached itself to you, you'd do well to figure out the why of it and help her move on. You don't need that."

"As opposed to the dog."

"That's different."

"How so?"

"On account of he's cute."

Jerry looked at the dog, who was sitting on the couch licking his privates. "You wouldn't be saying that if you knew what he was doing to your couch."

"Don't let him destroy our furniture!"

"I was kidding. But you might want to tip the cleaning lady a bit extra."

"Ewww."

"If I can't see or hear her, how am I supposed to help her?"

"I'm no expert, but since you've seen sprits in the past, it might not be you. It could have something to do with her death. If it was sudden or violent, the spirit might be confused by what happened to them."

"It's going to be difficult to find that out if she's not going to help me."

"It's all I've got, Jerry. Let me know if you get any clues and I'll try to help. You might want to check in with your little friend."

"Who, Max?"

"She seems pretty wired in to you. You said it yourself. It was Max that helped you save Alex."

"Good idea. I'll keep you in the loop." Jerry ended the call and nursed the rest of his beer while staring at the spirit, who'd yet to move from the far corner of the room. He lifted the can. "Want a beer?"

The apparition didn't move, but Gunter lifted his head, decided Jerry wasn't speaking to him, and continued his grooming. Jerry finished his beer, rinsed the can in the sink, and headed for the bedroom, pausing at the door to make sure he wasn't being followed. When neither ghost moved, Jerry closed the door behind him. He pulled a set of clothes from his seabag, placing them on the bed before stripping and taking his shaving kit to the bathroom. Jerry turned on the water and brought it to his face without waiting for it to get warm, then let it run as he lathered his face and used the razor to remove the cream. By the time he rinsed the remaining lather, the water was hot enough to fog the mirror. He wiped the towel across his freshly shaved face and froze. For a moment, the steamy reflection toyed with his mind, reminding him of his younger self – an image that looked very much like the ghostly replica of his brother. Jerry's jaw grew tight as he recalled the conversation with Joseph and the laughter in his brother's eyes when he admitted to letting Jerry carry the guilt of his own indiscretions. A lie that had robbed him of the rest of his childhood, stolen any semblance of a relationship with his father, and haunted him for the last seventeen years of his life.

Jerry sent his fist into the mirror, pulled his hand back, looked at the shattered image and pushed his hands through his hair. Gripping the back of his neck, he hugged his head with his elbows, rocking in place as tears rolled down his cheeks. It was so unfair. The lies. The guilt. The blame. Joseph's death. All just so damn unfair.

Jerry pulled his hands away from his head, saw the blood from his cut knuckles, and looked at the damage he'd done. *Shit.* At least the glass had remained within the frame. Easy enough to change out if a person knew what they were doing, which he did.

He leaned into the shower, turned on the water, and stepped inside. *Way to go, Jerry. You've just added vandalism to your resume.*

***

Jerry opened the door to the bedroom and tightened his grip on his towel. Gunter was lying on the bed. His ghostly hitchhiker sat next to him. Still feeling the sting of earlier emotions, Jerry's nostrils flared. "Both of you out, NOW!"

Both ghosts vanished. Okay, that was not exactly what he was going for, but it gave Jerry the privacy to get dressed without putting on a show. He reached for his pants and felt the tenderness in his knuckles.

Not broken, but it would serve as a constant reminder of his breakdown for days to come. He pulled on his pants and shirt, picked up his socks, then tossed them back on the bed before returning to the main room.

Gunter lay on the couch with his head on his paws. Though his eyes were open, the dog didn't bother acknowledging Jerry's return.

Jerry scanned the room for the hitchhiker, relaxing when he didn't see her. His relief was short-lived when he saw the shadowy form standing outside the kitchen window. Jerry sighed and looked to the ceiling. "Why me, lord?"

Not getting an answer, he opened the front door and addressed the apparition. "I meant get out of the bedroom. You may come back inside."

He stepped back as the ghostly visitor approached. She – Jerry was sure of that now – paused. He could almost make out a hand as the mist reached for him. He remained still as she caressed his cheek. A chill of recognition raced through him – though he didn't yet know the spirit's identity.

"I can help."

He felt an immense sadness course from the unseen fingers as she pulled her hand away.

Jerry sighed. "When you are ready, I am here."

Chapter Seven

After a restless night of dreams filled with memories from the past, Jerry woke with the knowledge of two certainties. A, he wasn't alone in the room – an obvious deduction since Gunter's snores were coming from the vicinity of the foot of the bed. B, the ghost that had attached herself to him was the spirit of his childhood friend.

Jerry drew in a long breath, blew it out slowly, then turned toward the shadowed form sitting on the edge of the hot tub. The apparition faded in and out several times before finally appearing to him in full form. She still had bright red hair, though it was easy to see she was much older than when he'd known her. She appeared to have outgrown many of the freckles that had captured his attention as a teen. There was a sadness about her, not just in the frown that tugged at her mouth but in the overall energy that surrounded her spirit. He started to get up but didn't want to scare her away, so he stayed where he was. "Hello, Patti."

She stood and moved closer to the bed. "You mean to say you can see me? I thought you could but wasn't sure."

"I can see you. I can hear you too."

"How? It's been so long. I thought I was invisible. I've tried talking to people, but no one could see me until now."

"It's a gift I have." He'd long debated that point, but it felt better to tell her it was a gift than insinuate speaking with her to be a curse.

She took a step closer. "Who are you?"

Well, that hurts. "You mean you don't know?"

Her forehead furrowed and she wrung her hands at her waist. "You seem familiar, but I can't place your name."

Jerry pulled up on his elbow and smiled. "Are you saying you had more than one person call you Patti Cakes?"

Recognition set in. "Jerry McNeal – the cutest boy in class."

Jerry felt his cheeks burn. He wanted to tell her it was good to see her too, but it wasn't – not like this. "What happened to you, Patti?"

"I was hoping you would tell me."

He took a deep breath and sat on the side of the bed facing her. "Do you know that you're dead?"

She continued to wring her hands then finally nodded her head. "I didn't want to believe it. But I knew better than to just think I was invisible."

"Do you know how it happened?"

She shook her head. "I've tried to remember.

Every time I try, I get scared."

"Were you ill? Maybe you got sick and that is how you died?"

"No. I don't think so." Patti's image faded and he knew she was struggling with his questions.

"An accident, maybe? Car wreck?"

"No, not that I remember." Patti's image faded in and out several more times. "You've got to help us, Jerry."

"Us?"

"You've got to help us, Jerry. You're the only one."

An image of Princess Leia talking to Obi-Wan Kenobi came to mind. Before Jerry could respond, Patti disappeared. Jerry lay back, intertwined his fingers under his head, and addressed the ceiling. "I don't know who the puppeteers are that are controlling my life, but I hope you're having fun."

Jerry's cell phone sounded his mother's ringtone and Gunter yawned a squeaky yawn. Jerry reached for the phone, checking the time before answering. "Good morning, Mom. You're up early."

"Can't help it. It comes with being old."

Jerry chuckled. "Then what's my excuse?"

"You're an old soul, Jerry. You always have been. Your dad and Marvin are picking their cornhole teams. Whose team do you want to be on?"

Jerry flexed his hand and winced. "Neither."

"Come on now, you have to pick a side."

That's easy. "I'll root for Dad, but I'm not playing."

"Come on, Jerry, I thought you and your dad were getting along well yesterday. It would mean a lot to him if you'd agree to be on his team."

"Mom, this is not about Dad. I hurt my hand and don't want to play."

"Hurt your hand how?"

"I may have used it to bust a mirror." He closed his eyes, waiting.

"Jerry Carter McNeal, what on earth were you thinking? Haven't you listened to a thing your grandmother taught you over the years? You have to know breaking a mirror will get you seven years of bad luck."

Jerry grimaced – it was true, his grandmother was the queen of superstitions. Still, it wasn't as if he'd benefited from years of playing by the so-called rules of don'ts. "As opposed to the last seventeen years?"

"What's that supposed to mean?"

"It's nothing, Mom. Just talking out loud."

"Are you okay, Jerry?"

"My hand's fine."

"I wasn't talking about your hand."

"I'm fine, Mom."

"So, no cornhole?"

"Not this year. Hey, Mom?"

"Yes, Jerry?"

"Do you remember that girl I liked in school?"

"Which one? There were so many of them."

"Patricia O'Conner. Her family moved to town when I was in the ninth grade."

"The little redhead?"

"That's the one."

"I seem to recall her mother was overprotective and pulled her from school before the end of the year."

A lot of good that did her. "Do you know whatever became of her?"

"Now that you mention it, I think I remember reading something about her in the paper. She was missing. I think they thought she might have run away or something. Ask Marvin. People are always telling him things. I swear, sometimes I think that man missed his calling. He should have run for mayor – probably still could – he knows more about what goes on in this town than anyone."

Jerry rolled his eyes upward. "That's just what Newport needs."

"Be nice, Jerry."

"I am being nice."

His mother sighed into the phone. "I guess I'd better go break the bad news to your father. At least it's better than taking Marvin's side out of spite."

Jerry thought of Patti's parents and the pain they must have endured not knowing what happened to their only daughter. While Joseph hadn't gone missing, the pain of his death had been just as difficult for his parents. Jerry hadn't been any comfort, as he'd taken the opportunity to distance himself even further from his family. He'd never been one for smart life choices, as was apparent by his decision to leave a perfectly good job so he could become a vagabond living out of his vehicle. *Suck it up, sad sack. Your vehicle cost as much as some houses.* The thought didn't help his sudden melancholy. Jerry tightened his grip on the phone. "I love you, Mom."

She hesitated. "Are you sure you're alright, Jerry?"

Not really. "I'm good. I'll see you in just a bit. Do you need me to bring anything?"

"No, I think we have everything covered."

"Okay, let me know if you change your mind. I'll see you soon."

Jerry clicked off the phone and turned to Gunter. "If I have to play nice with Uncle Marvin, that means you have to play nice with Sammy. Got it?"

Gunter growled.

"I'm serious."

Gunter smiled a doggy smile then growled once again.

Jerry laughed and rolled from the bed and headed to the bathroom. When he'd finished, he turned and stared at the shattered mirror. Jerry walked to the closet and took inventory of the tools on the small shelf. Not much, but everything he needed to make things right. He shut the closet door, thinking about Patti as he dressed. She couldn't recall being sick, nor could she remember being in an accident. His mom said the authorities presumed she'd run away. What would have given them that idea? From what he could remember, the girl had been happy. While her mother was overprotective, he couldn't recall the woman ever raising her voice. Her dad was okay, and her brothers seemed normal enough. Looking back, there was nothing that would have raised a red flag. So why had they given up looking for her? Could they have found her body if they had kept up the search? Patti was dead, of that he was sure. If she hadn't been sick or injured, that left one option. Patti was murdered. By whom? A family member? Was it someone in the house that convinced the police that she'd run away? Another thing he was sure of was that she was asking for help, and he intended to do whatever he could to help her find peace.

Jerry thought back to their brief conversation. She'd asked for his help – no, she said "help us." *Who's "us"?* Probably her family. If she wanted him to help them find closure, then it was highly unlikely they were responsible for her disappearance. *She's dead, Jerry – quit calling it a disappearance. Call it what it is – murder.*

Maybe that was why her spirit was still hanging around town. It could also be the reason she didn't follow him into the cemetery. Maybe since she wasn't buried there, she didn't think she belonged.

Jerry remembered what Savannah had said about reaching out to Max. He picked up his phone to call and opted to send a message instead. > *Hey Max, how are things?*

Jerry stared at the screen for a minute then pocketed the phone when he got no response. He returned to the bathroom, pulled the mirror from the wall, and carefully carried it to the outside trashcan – listening to the clink of glass as he tossed it inside.

"Sounds like someone had an accident."

Jerry turned toward the voice, which was attached to a brunette who, without a doubt, sported the nicest pair of legs he'd ever seen. He shrugged. "I didn't like what the bathroom mirror had to say."

She rocked back on her heels, brushed the hair behind her left ear with a ringless hand, and raised an eyebrow. "I hate when that happens. Pretty smart ditching the evidence. I hear the woman that owns the place is a cop."

Jerry smiled. "You must be Meg."

"I am. I was taking my morning walk and thought I'd see if you needed anything. I'm heading into town later; I can pick up a mirror if you'd like."

"I'll take care of it. I need to pick up a few more things while I'm at it." He gave her a sly smile. "I may need help drinking some of those beers later."

"Says the guy who took out a mirror for just

looking at him the wrong way."

"And yet you're still standing here."

Meg laughed a carefree laugh. "You're barefoot. I figure I can outrun you."

Jerry shook his head. "Not smart."

"What?"

"Giving away your escape plan."

"Yes, well, don't you go counting me out just yet. I still have a trick or two up my sleeve. And before you go getting any ideas, you'd be best to know that my daddy didn't raise no sissy girl. I've got to be getting along. You going to be in the area long?"

He hadn't planned on it, but that was before Patti showed up. Now he felt obligated to help her remember what happened to her and help her and her parents find peace. "A few more days at least."

"Make sure to pick up some antibiotic ointment while you're in town. That hand of yours is starting to look a bit angry."

As she turned to leave, Jerry noted that Meg looked just as good from the back as she had from the front. He also was very much aware of the pistol she had tucked into the waistband of her shorts.

Chapter Eight

Jerry arrived at Marvin's cabin just after nine to find a line of cars parked along the oversized driveway, some spilling onto the yard. Jerry backed onto the lawn, taking care to park far enough away from the cabin to leave without issue. It wasn't that he planned on leaving early. It was the cop in him that always had a plan. While he might no longer be a state trooper, the training was ingrained – assess the threats and always give yourself an out. Back into parking spots to allow for an easier departure. Case each room upon entry and know where your exits are. Never close the gap between cars when in a line of traffic, as it allows criminals to box you in.

Gunter pushed his head through the glass window. Jerry laughed at the absurdity.

"Yo, dog?"

Gunter pulled his head inside. Jerry used the button on the door to lower the window, and Gunter stuck his head through the opening. Jerry was just about to shut off the engine when the dashboard lit up, alerting him to Max's call. "Hey, Max, what's up?"

"Mom's on my case as usual."

"Anything I can help with?"

"Nah. You know, just normal mom and kid stuff."

"You're an old soul, Max."

"Is that good?"

Jerry laughed. "The heck if I know, but my grandmother and my mom used to tell me the same thing."

"Then I'll take that as a compliment."

"How's the journaling coming? Any new leads?" Jerry saw movement from the second-floor deck and looked to see his mom staring over the side rail at him. He motioned that he was on the phone and held up a finger to let her know he'd be another moment.

"My ghost has red hair."

Jerry looked at the dash, wondering if he'd heard correctly. "Wait, what did you say, Max?"

"Yep. I thought she needed my help because she was going to be murdered, but I think it's already happened. So that makes her a ghost."

Jerry's mind walked through the possibilities. Had that been their connection all along? Had Max somehow dialed in on Patti? It wouldn't be the first time Max had picked up on something connected to him. Could it be that simple? That each of their spirits had red hair couldn't be coincidental. Could it? "Max, you said your ghost has red hair. Are you sure?"

"Pretty sure. Is that bad?"

"Bad, no, not at all." Jerry fought hard to keep from feeding the girl information. "Before, you said she appeared to you. Have you seen her in person or just in your dreams?"

"She visits my dreams. I thought I saw a ghost before, but my mom told me I didn't, so I don't know for sure."

Jerry did not doubt that the ghost Max claimed to see was real. Children often see ghosts; it is the parents that convince them otherwise. Jerry had the opposite problem. His grandmother encouraged him to see what others could not. "Do you remember the first time you keyed on the lady in your dreams?"

"It was last summer. That's when she started visiting my dreams. I wasn't scared at first, because I've had visits before. Then I started feeling she was going to be murdered, and that scared me because I wanted to help her. That's when I broke down and told my mom. I think it scared her too because she told her friend, Carrie. It's a good thing she did because Carrie was the one who was visiting Gettysburg and read about you in the newspaper. That's when Mom wrote you the letter."

Jerry sighed his frustration. The timing didn't fit. Max's ghost appeared before she or her mother even knew of his existence. Unless Patti had figured out a way to use Max to get a message to him, then this was all just a huge coincidence. *It's pretty thin, Jerry.*

Jerry rubbed his hand over his head, wincing at the pain in his still tender knuckles.

"Are you still there, Jerry?"

"I'm here. I was just trying to sort out the puzzle."

"That's a good analogy. The lady with green eyes and red hair. The bell. It's all just a giant puzzle. Is that what it's like solving police work? Figuring out a puzzle?"

"That is exactly what it is. You put everything together to help solve the case. Sometimes it's like you went to the thrift shop and bought your puzzle. You have all these pieces, only to discover someone has added pieces that don't belong. So, you set them aside. Sometimes those pieces work their way back into the puzzle, but not always. Have you ever watched any police shows where they put the pictures up on the wall and try to connect them?"

"Yes."

"The detectives do that so they can look at the whole picture at once. They look at those pieces every day. Then one day, they might turn their head a certain way and see something they didn't see all the other times they looked."

"Cool." Max grew quiet for a moment. "Are you okay, Jerry?"

Jerry smiled. "I'm good."

"But you hurt your hand."

"It's nothing."

"Did you really hit your brother?"

Jerry sighed. "No, I hit a mirror while thinking about my brother."

"Did you break it?"

"No, my hand is fine."

"I was talking about the mirror. It's bad luck to do that."

"You sound like my mom."

"Are you still mad at him?"

Good question. "I don't know."

"I don't think you should be mad. Your brother's a kid. Kids do stupid things."

Max had a valid point. Joseph was only fourteen when he screwed up. And only twenty-one when he died. Still, the conversation with Joseph was too fresh to revisit. He decided to cast a net to see if Max would key on Patti. "Listen, I've got to be going. I've got to meet my friend Patti. Keep working on your puzzle. Let me know if you come up with anything."

"Okay, Jerry, I will. See ya."

"Later, Max." Jerry was almost hesitant to end the call but pressed the button when Max didn't take the bait. Jerry replayed their conversation as he drummed his uninjured fingers on the steering wheel. *What are you missing, Jerry? Maybe there's nothing to miss. There are only so many natural hair colors to choose from. Is it so far-reaching to have two ghosts with the same hair color? If they'd both been brunettes, you probably wouldn't have given it a second thought. So why think that way just because Max said the woman in her dreams had red hair? Give it a rest, McNeal. It's just a coincidence. Accept it and move on. But what if it isn't? What would Granny say?*

"I'd ask you if you are going to sit here and argue with yourself all day or if you are going to go join your family."

Jerry looked in the mirror as Gunter disappeared from the front seat and reappeared in the next row, welcoming the woman with eager doggy kisses. Jerry smiled. "Good morning, Granny. I was beginning to think you'd forgotten your promise."

She gave the dog some attention then appeared in the seat beside him. "When have I ever not kept my promise to you?"

He shrugged. "When you died."

"Couldn't be helped." She tapped the left side of her chest. "The old ticker gave out."

"The doctors said…"

"I don't give a rat's ass what the doctors said. It was my body, so I should know what happened to it."

"I suppose that is true. So you're telling me that you remember dying?"

"Of course. I'm dead, not senile."

Jerry thought of his conversation with Patti. "Do all spirits normally recall what happened to them?"

She considered this a moment. "No, not always."

"What would cause a ghost…"

His grandmother put up a hand to stop him. "Spirit, Jerry. We prefer to be called spirits."

"Okay, spirit. What would cause a spirit not to remember their death?"

"Denial. Fear. Trauma."

"Trauma? Like if someone were murdered?"

She nodded. "The dead can suffer from PTSD too, you know."

Great. Something to look forward to in the afterlife. "No, I didn't know."

"The spirit is supposed to learn something during their time on earth. But some things are better left behind. A body that didn't work properly. A life that didn't fulfill. A traumatic death."

"I can understand that. But what if the ghost – sorry, spirit – can't move on until they remember?"

"You're talking about your friend."

"She asked for my help. She can't recall what happened to her. How do I help her if she can't remember?"

Her gaze fell to his injured hand and a sadness touched her eyes. "You want to fix your friend's problems, but you choose to run from those that plague you."

"I don't have any problems."

She narrowed her eyes at him. "The hell you don't. You've spent the last seventeen years living with guilt. Just look what it did to you. You have panic attacks. You run when things don't go your way. Now you've replaced the guilt with anger. I'm here to tell you that anger will rot at your soul. You must forgive Joseph. If you don't, that anger will fester until it drives you mad." She looked at him as if willing him to understand. "Marvin was not always the man you see. He had so much to offer. You and he are a lot alike, Jerry. You don't see it, but I know it to be true."

Jerry felt his jaw tense. "I'm nothing like him."

She touched his hand. "Your friend isn't the only one who must remember."

Jerry pulled away from her touch and slammed his hand against the steering wheel, instantly regretting his action. "Why can't I just be normal?"

"Because you're destined to be so much more."

"Don't I get a choice?"

She lightly took hold of his injured hand. Instantly, the pain lessened. "We all have a choice. You agreed to this long ago."

"What if I've changed my mind and don't want to do this anymore?"

"Don't say things in haste you will later regret." She let go of his hand and nodded toward the house. "They're waiting for you."

"Are you coming?"

"I'm always near."

Jerry opened the door, expecting Gunter to follow, only to discover the cab of the SUV empty. He turned and saw the dog standing behind him, tail wagging his excitement. "Remember what I said about teasing the dog."

Gunter lowered into a playful bow.

Jerry chuckled then remembered his mom was watching. He looked to the balcony in hopes she'd grown weary of waiting, only to discover his father had joined her. *Great.* His father said something he couldn't hear as his mother waved him forward.

Jerry rolled his neck as Gunter glued himself to his side. He opened the door to the basement level and was met with laughter. A cluster of children stood in front of the television, imitating the movements of a dance video on the screen. Joseph stood in the middle of the group, laughing and dancing as if they knew he was standing amongst them. His spirit looked up and his smile wavered. At that moment, Jerry knew Max was right. Joseph hadn't acted in malice. The boy's behavior was nothing more than that of a child who'd yet to grow up.

Jerry smiled and gave a slight nod of the chin.

Joseph mirrored his action then went back to playing with his nieces and nephews.

Gunter hesitated for a moment, then followed Jerry up the stairs. Several women sat in the living room, talking in hushed tones. Jerry waved, then took a Budweiser from the fridge and headed to the back deck.

"Jerry, my boy, what's this I hear about you not wanting to join our cornhole game?" Marvin yelled the moment he stepped on the deck. Granny was standing next to her brother, peering at Jerry as if reminding him of his promise to be nice.

Jerry held up his injured hand. "Not this year, Uncle."

Marvin opened his mouth and his sister placed her hand on his shoulder. Marvin closed his mouth and acknowledged the gesture by placing his hand on top of hers. Jerry stared at his uncle. There was no doubt Marvin had felt the touch as sure as if she'd been alive. *How could that be?*

He remembered his grandmother's words. *You and he are a lot alike, Jerry. You don't see it, but I know it to be true.* Jerry realized he was staring at the man and turned away. A mistake, as his mother furrowed her brow.

"Are you alright, Jerry? You're looking a bit pale."

Jerry forced a smile. "I'm good, Mom."

His father had been in the midst of a story when he arrived and continued with his tale.

As Jerry listened, he watched his grandmother approach Lori and place a kiss on the side of her cheek. When his mother failed to respond to the gesture, his grandmother moved on. The lack of acknowledgment saddened him. And he knew at that moment what it was like to be normal. Would he really be happy at never seeing or speaking with his grandmother again? Though the woman had been dead for years, he could still feel her when she touched him. Still hear her when she spoke. Jerry brushed his hand over the top of his skull as he remembered her words. *I'm always near*. Was he actually willing to give that up?

Gunter leaned against his leg as if reminding him that he too was real only to him and others that had the gift. Jerry felt comfort in the dog's weight and realized he'd come to enjoy the dog's presence. He lowered his hand, his fingers grazing the fur of his ghostly companion. Instantly, he no longer wished to be normal. Not if it meant giving up the comforts of the unseen touch.

Chapter Nine

Jerry leaned against the tree watching his dad toss beanbags onto the cornhole board. He'd positioned himself so that he could easily talk to his dad yet quietly observe his uncle. Though he'd spent most of his life avoiding the man, at the moment, he wanted nothing more than to get his uncle alone so he could speak with him about the secret he hid.

Marvin threw the last beanbag, sinking it along with another that had been teetering in the opening. "That's the game, Wayne. Unless you can convince Jerry here to join you in another."

Jerry had reluctantly agreed to join using his left hand after one of his nephews failed to help his dad gather any points during the first game. Jerry was about to agree to the match-up when his dad begged off.

Marvin agreed and motioned to the kids who swooped in, gathering the bags and calling teams. Marvin turned to his son-in-law and pointed to the cooler. "Robert, bring that along. Leave it out here and these boys will be drunk by sundown."

Jerry saw looks of disappointment on the boys'

faces and silently commended his uncle for his foresight.

Marvin moved up beside him and held out his hand. "Jerry, my man, I need you to read my palm."

Jerry ignored the hand and continued to walk to the house.

"Oh, come on, son. Give it a try."

Jerry slid a look to his father, whose face remained noncommittal. "Actually, Uncle, I was hoping you could tell me something."

Marvin pulled his hand back. "What would you like to know?"

I want to know why you never told me you have the gift. Jerry kept that thought to himself for the time being. The fact that he'd never learned of his uncle's gift meant the man wished it to remain a secret. "Do you remember a girl by the name of Patti O'Conner?"

Marvin frowned and scratched at his head. "Patti O'Conner? Nope, doesn't sound familiar."

"Patricia O'Conner. I brought her to the house once or twice. Her family lived over on North Street."

Marvin's face lit up. "The little redhead girl with all the freckles?"

At the mention of her name, Patti showed up. Jerry nodded.

"Isn't she the woman that went missing?" Robert asked over his shoulder.

Jerry looked at Robert. "She is. Did you know her?"

"No. I just remember seeing a poster hanging on the door at Pit Pass. Pretty lady."

Marvin tapped his forehead. "As I recall, her parents offered a hefty reward for any information. Don't seem to remember the police ever having any leads."

"Maybe they quit looking too soon." Jerry raised his voice to get his uncle's attention. "What do you think, Marvin?"

Marvin started to answer then stopped, looking over Jerry's shoulder at Patti. He blinked several times then shook off the shock. "I reckon so."

The group reached the deck and Jerry took hold of Marvin's arm. "Can I speak to you a moment, Uncle?"

Marvin smiled. "Want to exchange war stories?"

"No." The word came out a little louder than he'd intended, and Marvin looked as if he were about to bolt up the stairs. "I just have a few questions for you."

Marvin sighed and started walking to a bench that sat under the tree a few feet away. He sat and Jerry joined him. "What's on your mind, Jerry?"

Jerry had rolled the question over in his mind at least a hundred times during the course of the day. How best to ask without putting his uncle on defense. In the end, he opted for the direct approach.

"Why didn't you ever tell me you have the gift?"

"Gift? I don't have no gift for you."

Stay calm, Jerry. "You felt Granny put her hand on your shoulder. I know because I saw you touch her hand. You saw Patti and Gunter too."

"Gunter?"

"The dog."

Marvin blew out a shaky breath. "Okay, I wasn't sure on that one, but I thought maybe when no one else mentioned him…"

"He was a police dog – got shot in the line of duty and for some reason thinks he belongs with me." Jerry thought about telling him that Granny and Joseph sent him but didn't want to complicate the situation. "So why didn't you tell me?"

Marvin laughed. "When was I supposed to tell you? During one of our friendly chats? Hell, boy, this is the first time I can recall you talking to me without looking like you wanted to spit in my eye."

Truth. "That's because I have a hard time stomaching your lies." Jerry ran a hand over his head. "I've been in war – seen the horrors and know what it does to a man. To have you belittle that by claiming to have served. Yes, I've loathed you for it."

"And yet you're sitting here now."

"That's because I am trying to understand. Why would a man go through life telling lies?"

"Because they don't feel like lies to me. Like

right now, I could tell you the names of every man I served with. I could describe every mission I've ever been on."

"That's because you've seen it on television or heard it on the news."

Marvin turned and looked Jerry in the eye. "Doc – real name Harrold Mattingly. Boz – real name Ricky DuPriest. Turner – Daniel. Delong – Ethan. I can name the ones we lost if you'd like. I could also give you specifics of our missions."

We? Marvin hadn't served with any of those men. Oh, they were real men alright – each of the men Marvin had listed were Marines Jerry had served with. The thing was, he had never mentioned them to anyone – not even in the letters he sent home. Jerry worked to remain calm. Even if the man were a computer geek – which he most certainly was not – there was no way his uncle could be privy to any of that information. "How?"

Marvin shook his head. "I wish I knew."

"Sorry, Uncle, but that answer isn't good enough."

"I can hear it. In your mind."

"You're telling me you can read minds?"

Marvin chuckled.

"There's nothing funny about this."

"No, I guess you're right. I was just laughing at the irony. You're ready to accept that I see ghosts but question the fact that I can sometimes hear your thoughts."

Jerry remembered visualizing shooting the man and felt the heat in his cheeks.

Marvin winked. "Glad you only imagined it. Doubt I would survive something like that."

"Why didn't you say anything?"

"What would you have me say?"

"You let me and the whole family think you're crazy."

"Not everyone. Some know the truth."

"But why keep me in the dark?" *I would have understood.*

"No, you wouldn't."

Jerry realized he hadn't voiced that last sentence out loud.

"Do you remember the game we used to play?"

"No."

"It was a guessing game. You would think of something and I would tell you what you were thinking."

"I played a similar game with Granny but don't remember playing it with you."

"It was a long time ago. Anyway, one day, you were upset and I knew that you'd gone into your parents' bedroom and found your daddy's gun."

"I don't remember that."

"Well, you did. I think you were around eight at the time. You didn't do anything with it, just looked at it and put it back. And instead of telling you that I knew what you'd done, I told your dad—only instead of fessing up to it, you lied, and Wayne, he tanned your backside a good one. You were so mad at me, you told me you hated me and you refused to play the game after that. Matter of fact, you refused to come around me unless someone else was there. I guess you figured I couldn't read your mind if you weren't alone."

Jerry sighed. "I still don't understand why you repeat the stories. I mean, everyone knows you were never in the war. Do you prefer people to think you're crazy?"

"When I was a young boy, I was just like you. I could feel things. Know something was going to happen before it took place."

"So, you were like Granny."

"Yes, only I didn't have anyone like your grandmother to coddle me and tell me it was alright to be different. I had a pop who preferred to beat the devil out of a boy for what he perceived as telling lies. He'd call me a snake charmer and he'd lay down the law with his belt."

"Wait, then why did Granny get away with it?"

"Because Granny was a girl. Menfolk of that time didn't pay no attention to what came out of a girl child's mouth. So your grandmother got to grow up being normal and I, well, I had to live a lie."

That he'd called his sister's gift normal came as a shock. Jerry had always thought otherwise.

"After the accident with the tractor, something changed. I could hear people's thoughts. And well, my daddy didn't like that I could tell him what was going on in his mind. But he was so scared I would tell someone that he started being a little nicer to me. When I'd say something, he'd tell people I was a little off in the head because of the accident. People don't always pay no mind to a simpleton. Since they didn't think I was too smart, I was able to use that to my advantage. And since I could read their thoughts, I used that to my advantage as well. When something didn't go as planned, I would fall back on my war stories and, well, they'd leave me be. They'd think I was crazy. Only while I was talking, I was listening. When things went wrong on the job, I'd sue. Since I could get inside their heads, I knew which ones were likely to settle without putting up a fuss. When they were lying on the witness stand, I'd have my attorney call them on it."

Jerry blew out a whistle. "Crazy like a fox."

"I wish I would have kept my intuition. If I had, maybe I would have known what was going to happen that day with Joseph. I couldn't do anything about that, but I could make it right for you. That construction foreman knew he'd cut corners. Why, he showed up on the site before they'd even cleared the wreckage and was going down the list in his mind of everything he'd done wrong. Man, was he surprised when my lawyer hit him with a suit that listed everything in the exact order the man had thought it. I couldn't bring Joseph back, but I could use what I had to make the man pay."

Jerry looked at the cabin. "Seems you made out pretty well in the deal."

"You got a fair share yourself," Marvin reminded him.

"I didn't ask for any of that money."

"No, your brother did."

"You spoke to Joseph after his death."

"You're not the only one with the gift, remember? Joseph told me to make the man pay and told me you were to get the money. That was a given, because he'd seen to that in his will. But he seemed to think he owed you something. I tried to read him to see what that was, but he blocked me from seeing. But now I see you know what he was upset about. That boy loved you. Even after you went away, he would go on and on about his big brother Jerry. Only he died before he could tell you himself. He thought that by seeing you were taken care of, you would know how much you meant to him."

Jerry sniffed and realized he was crying. *Shit.*

"It's okay, son. Crying doesn't make a man a sissy."

Jerry wiped the tears from his eyes. "I've wasted so much of my life taking the blame for others' actions and hating people I had no business hating."

"Not everyone has the luxury of seeing through lies."

"That doesn't make it any easier."

"I don't suppose it does. You'll figure it out."

"Figure what out?"

"Your life. Betty Lou always felt your gift was your destiny."

"Granny had more faith in me than I have in myself." Jerry frowned. "Why didn't Granny ever set me straight about you?"

"Betty Lou was an old soul and considered you one too. She was convinced that you had to find your own way. That meant letting you learn your life's lessons when the time was right."

It was weird. He'd spent so much time loathing the man, he didn't realize how much he and his sister were alike. "Granny told me if I came here, I would find the answers I seek. But I'm even more confused than ever."

Marvin smiled. "Care to play a game?"

"You going to read my mind?"

"No, but I'd like to pick your brain."

"Go ahead. It's not like I can stop you."

"Why'd you leave the Marines?"

"Because even though I knew when something was going to happen, I couldn't do anything about it."

"And the police force. How'd you handle that?"

"That was different. When I went to pull a car

over, I knew if the person inside was just having a crappy day or if they were a habitual liar feeding me a line of bull." Jerry looked at his uncle. "No offense."

"None taken."

"I had a great sergeant who knew about my gift and let me run with it. I didn't take advantage, but some on the force got bent out of shape about the perceived favoritism. And I guess it was to a point, but I did good. I saved lives and made a difference."

"And yet you left."

"Things were changing. The sergeant was getting pushback from his boss and I knew there would come a time when I would know something was going to happen but couldn't do anything about it. It would have been the Marines all over again."

"How long have you been off the job?"

"A few weeks."

"But it isn't what you thought, is it?"

"No. I mean, I've helped a lot of people, but there are just as many people who I haven't helped. I feel like everyone is screaming for my attention and yet I'm powerless to help them all."

"What if I told you that you don't have to?"

"I feel like this is the exact opposite of what Granny taught me. Why have this gift if I'm not supposed to use it?"

Marvin shook his head. "I'm not telling you not to use your gift. I'm telling you that you need to focus it a bit more. You're not a cop anymore. So stop doing cop stuff. Oh, you can do the occasional good deed and stop big things. But let the cops focus on the petty crime."

"What should I be focusing on?"

"Your gift."

"No offense, Uncle, but I feel like you're talking in circles."

"What can you do that most people can't?"

"Know when something's going to happen."

"Besides that."

"See and talk with the dead."

"Bingo!"

"I'm not following you."

"Maybe that is your calling."

"Still not connecting."

"Most everyone can help the living in some way somehow. But it would take someone with a real gift to help the dead. Take your friend over there."

Jerry had been so caught up in their conversation, he'd completely forgotten about Patti, who was wandering through the yard with Gunter by her side.

"She's been dead for years and no one has been able to help her find peace."

It was true. Patti had asked for his help. She'd even told him he was the only one. "How am I supposed to help her?"

"You were a cop; you'll figure it out."

For the first time in as long as he could

remember, things made sense. *Could it really be that easy?*

"Easy, no. Fulfilling, yes."

"Okay, I know you can do it, but that doesn't make it less weird."

Marvin smiled. "Would you rather hear a war story?"

Jerry shook his head. "I'm good with the mind-reading."

Chapter Ten

If not for Patti's ghostly reflection staring him in the face each time he looked in the rearview mirror, Jerry would consider himself to be on the top of the world. Even his hand felt better thanks to the Motrin he'd taken throughout the day. Vitamin M, as it was referred to in the military, since it was handed out for everything from a stuffy nose to a bullet wound.

The conversation with Marvin had not only given him a new direction but had removed the anger he was harboring against the man. While he didn't care to listen to any of the stories that came from his uncle's head, Jerry no longer felt his skin crawl at the mere mention of the man's name. That he'd gone through his life hating his uncle even more than he'd hated himself told him just how messed up his childhood had been. *Nothing to be done about that now, Jerry. Best to put it to bed and get on with your life.*

Jerry glanced at Patti, who hadn't spoken since asking for his help. "You're awfully quiet."

Patti answered by disappearing.

Gunter yawned. Jerry shook his head. "What?

All I said was she was being quiet. It would be easier if she would talk. Even more so if she could remember what happened to her."

Gunter growled.

"I know she might not want to remember, but I'm not sure how to help her if she doesn't." Jerry pulled into the Lowes parking lot and glanced in the mirror to ensure Patti was gone. Better to have her leave on her own than to tell her she had to find another ride home. Jerry parked and got out, expecting Gunter to follow. When the K-9 didn't move, he shut the door and went inside without him. Jerry found a flat cart and headed for the bathroom section. He wrestled an elongated chair-height toilet onto the cart and then went in search of vanities. He didn't have to struggle with indecision as he'd recently renovated the small bathroom in his garage apartment in Pennsylvania and picked the same fixtures he'd chosen for his own space. He was thankful the cabin shower had already been updated. Not only did he not have the tools needed for the job, his hand – though better – wasn't up to laying tile. Jerry found the vanity he was looking for and pushed the cart next to the box.

"Need some help?"

He turned and saw a store employee standing behind him. Jerry put a name to the face without looking at the man's name tag. Brian McCampbell – the boy had had the locker next to him all through school. Though you couldn't tell it from the balding head and dad body, Brian had been one of the pretty boys. One of the most popular boys with the girls, the man now stood in front of him with a bloated face and a red apron. Brian's eyebrow went up. "Jerry McNeal? What are you doing here? I thought you'd left town."

And I thought you were voted most likely to succeed. Easy, Jerry, at least the man has a job. Jerry smiled. "Brian."

"I heard you'd moved out of town," Brian repeated as he nodded to the toilet box sitting on the cart. "Are you back?"

"No, just came home for a quick visit. I'm doing a couple of minor updates to a friend's cabin while in town."

Brian walked around and helped Jerry lift the vanity onto the cart. "So, what'cha been up to? Still in the Marines? No wait, I think I remember your uncle saying you're a cop now."

"I was. I'm doing a little freelance work now."

"Construction?"

Jerry ran his hand over his head, searching for an answer. "Private investigator."

"No shit? Who do you work for?"

Jerry said the first thing that came to mind. "Ghostbusters."

Brian laughed. "That's what I always liked about you, Jerry. You're a funny guy."

Only I was being serious. "That's me."

"So, what do you investigate? I bet it's cheating spouses? Boy, I could have used you when I was married. Pam, she's my ex, bled me dry. She spent every penny we had in savings and then ran off with Randy Hinkle. Do you remember him from school?"

Yep. Football jock that thought he was God's gift to women. Jerry nodded.

"Freaking jerk owns a gym in Nashville. Anyway, that's why I'm here. I'm working two jobs to keep from losing my house."

Way to judge the man, Jerry. "Sorry to hear about your troubles, but I'm not that kind of investigator. I'm more of a missing persons kind of guy."

Brian scratched his head. "Boy, that's some cool shit. We could have used you around here a few years ago when Patti O'Conner went missing."

Jerry raised an eyebrow. "You knew Patti."

A blush crept over Brian's cheeks. "That's right. You used to date her too."

"Too?"

"We had a thing. It didn't last long – her mom was too pushy."

"Pushy, how?"

"She liked me." Brian laughed. "Not in that way. She liked me for Patti. I mean, I liked Patti alright, but when her mom started planning our dates and talking about us getting married one day, it was just way too much. So I broke it off."

"You should feel honored. When Patti's mom found out she and I liked each other, she pulled Patti out of school."

"Oh man, seriously?"

"Yep. I guess her mom didn't see me as the marrying type." Jerry held up his left hand and sighed. "I suppose she was right."

"Never been?"

"Nope. Never found anyone I wanted to spend the rest of my life with."

A frown tugged at Brian's mouth. "I thought I had."

Shit. The guy looks like he's going to cry. Think, Jerry. "So, from what I've heard, the police stopped looking for Patti. Any idea why they think she ran off."

Brian looked over his shoulder before answering. "I may have had a hand in that."

Any sympathy Jerry had for the guy dissipated. "You? Why would you tell them that?"

"Because it's true. Patti told me so. Apparently, you weren't the only guy her mother ran off. Patti hated how controlling her mother was and was ready to make a new start." Brian stood taller and tried unsuccessfully to pull in his gut. "Patti was not happy when we broke up because I was the one guy her mother didn't have a problem with her dating. I saw her at the Fox and Hound a couple of days before she disappeared. Patti was sitting at a table alone and I stopped for a moment to say hello. She told me she'd met someone and he'd promised to take her away — told her she'd never have to step foot in this town again."

A chill crept over Jerry. "Any idea who this guy was? Someone local or a person she'd met online perhaps?"

"She didn't say. To be honest, I didn't ask many questions. That was before me and Pam split, and I didn't want my wife grilling me about talking to another woman." Brian let out a sigh. "Jesus, did that sound as pathetic to you as it does to me?"

It did. Jerry clapped Brian on the shoulder. Instantly, he pictured the man in a recliner hooked up to IVs. Only Jerry knew the therapy would be too late. *Shit!*

"You okay there, Jerry? You don't look so good."

Jerry stared the man in the eye without removing his hand. "Do you remember why people used to give me a hard time in school?"

Brian swallowed. "Because some of the kids thought you were as crazy as your uncle?"

Brutal but true. Jerry nodded. "There was some truth to it. Not the crazy part, but that I know things before they happen."

Brian glanced at Jerry's battered hand, then searched the ceiling — presumably for a security camera — and Jerry realized the guy was trembling under his touch. "So you knew about me and Patti? You're not going to beat me up, are you, Jerry?"

Shit. Jerry released him. "No, I'm not going to beat you up. Listen, I don't know how to say this other than just putting it out there. You need to make an appointment with the doctor. Tell him there is something wrong and you need him to do some tests."

Brian giggled a nervous laugh. "What kind of tests?"

Jerry ran his hand over his head. "That's the thing of it. I don't know. You have cancer. I don't know what kind. I just know if you don't get after it now, it may be too late by the time they find it."

Brian looked to the front of the building. "Should I go to the ER?"

Jerry placed his hand on the man's shoulder more to calm the man than to get any further reading. "No, just schedule an appointment with your doctor."

Brian bobbed his head up and down. "Okay, I'll call first thing in the morning."

As soon as he said it, Jerry's feeling of certain death waned. Jerry withdrew his hand. "That's good, Brian."

"You need anything else?" Brian nodded toward the cart. "For your project?"

"I still have a few things on my list." Jerry hesitated. He'd been debating surprising the girls with a washer and dryer but didn't think it would fit in the Durango with the rest of the items. He leveled a look at Brian. "What's the possibility of getting a stackable washer and dryer delivered tomorrow?"

Brian raised an eyebrow. "This wasn't all some ploy to get me to say yes, was it?"

Jerry looked the man in the eye. "I wish it was, my friend. I truly wish it was."

Brian smiled a determined smile. "I'll see that you get it even if I have to deliver it myself."

***

Unable to sleep, Jerry stayed up most of the night working in the bathroom. He switched out the dated black toilet for a clean white water-saving chair-height throne. He removed the old vanity and replaced it with a black cabinet with a white marble top with thin black veins running through it. Lastly, he hung a new black-framed mirror over the sink to replace the one he'd broken. As he stared at his reflection, he couldn't help thinking how much his moment of anger had cost him.

Jerry straightened the frame and surveyed the rest of his handiwork. Except for the worn towels, which hung on the towel rack, the bathroom was now fully updated. Everything blended well and would bring a smile to Savannah's and Alex's faces the next time they visited the cabin. That knowledge made the lack of sleep and money he'd spent entirely worth it.

He heard a backup alarm and went to the front

door. Gunter stood on the porch barking at the new arrival. Two men climbed out, circling to the back of the truck, unaware of the K-9's ghostly alarm.

"You should name this cabin and put out a sign so people know there is a drive out there."

Jerry eyed the man. "I do that, I might get more visitors. Truth be told, I rather like my privacy."

"Understood. But the next time you get a delivery, you might want to warn them so they don't pass up the place."

"I'll keep that in mind."

The driver looked at his clipboard. "Says here you have a stackable unit coming."

"That's right."

"Where do you want it?"

Jerry took a chance. "Hooked up inside."

The driver frowned at the clipboard. "It doesn't say anything about installation."

Jerry rocked back on his heels. "Simple job. Set it in place and hook up a couple of hoses. Fifty bucks?"

The driver looked at his partner. "What do you say we have a steak for lunch?"

The second man nodded his agreement. "Beats the hell out of a peanut butter sandwich."

The driver smiled. "Buddy, you've got yourself a deal." He lifted the back gate on the cargo box, climbed inside, and found the container he was looking for. He slid the unit to the tailgate then used a lever to lower them to ground level. Both men took hold of the box, easily carrying it inside. Start to finish, it took them twenty minutes to take it inside, unbox the unit, and make sure everything was hooked up and running. Jerry got an added bonus when the driver decided to take home the black toilet to use as a yard planter, and he further convinced the man to take the outdated vanity as well.

With the new stuff put in place and the old stuff gone, Jerry enjoyed a great sense of satisfaction as he watched Gunter chase the truck down the driveway. The K-9 paused halfway, his tail stiffening. He sniffed the air several times and the tail began to wag as he raced down the driveway. Jerry started to call him back so he didn't run off, then laughed at the absurdity. If the dog were to run into a bear, the worst thing that would happen was the bear would get scared and run off.

Jerry sat in the swing, enjoying the solitude of his surroundings. He liked that the cabin was nestled within the mountains and enjoyed the songbirds serenading him from the thick canopy of nearby trees. If he'd been looking to settle down, he couldn't think of a better place to bide his time. A piece of him wanted nothing more than to call Savannah and Alex and ask if they'd be interested in selling the cabin. A bigger part of him knew better than to get too comfortable. The conversation with Marvin had struck a chord. After all these years, he was ready to admit that his grandmother had been right when telling him he was destined for more. He would begin his new mission by helping Patti find out what had happened to her. The only problem was, while he knew what had to be done, he hadn't the slightest clue where to begin.

Chapter Eleven

Jerry was still sitting on the porch enjoying the solitude when his cell phone rang, his mom's ringtone disturbing the silence. "Hi, Mom. How's the trip?"

"We haven't left yet. Your father decided to hang around a few more hours. We'd love to meet for an early lunch."

The mere mention of food had his stomach rumbling its agreement. "Sure. Where do you want to meet?"

"How about Family Farm?"

"Works for me." Jerry checked the time on his phone. "Give me about forty-five minutes."

"Okay, son. See you there."

Jerry looked for Gunter before going inside and taking a quick shower. When he was finished, he dried off with the ratty towels and made a mental note to pick up a couple of new ones while he was in town. Jerry chuckled. If things didn't work out in the ghost business, he could always switch to bathroom remodeling.

Jerry dressed, started a load of laundry, and

headed outside. He was nearly to the Durango when he felt someone watching him. A quick scan of the area proved him right – Patti sat on the swing with Gunter lying at her feet. The sight of them together tugged at his heart. For a moment, he wondered if things would have turned out different for them both if Patti's mother hadn't pulled her out of school.

Don't go down that road, Jerry. You were just kids, and it was seventeen years ago. Your life is messed up enough as it is. Stop playing what ifs.

Jerry walked back to where Patti was sitting. "I'm meeting my parents for lunch. After that, we will try to figure out what happened to you."

She nodded without speaking.

"You're welcome to ride with me."

Patti disappeared. When Jerry turned, he saw her sitting in the passenger seat. Jerry opened the driver's side door and Gunter sailed past him. The K-9 hesitated momentarily before moving to the backseat. Jerry slid into the driver's seat and looked at his passengers. A normal, happy little family heading to town. Only there wasn't anything normal about any of them, and the spirit sitting beside him was anything but happy.

Jerry stretched a hand and caressed the back of his neck. "I ran into Brian McCampbell in the store yesterday. He seemed to know a lot about you."

Patti's image faded in and out several times.

"He said the two of you used to be a thing."

Patti faded then reappeared as a ghostly shadow.

"He said you were upset when he broke up with you."

Patti returned full force and turned to him, eyes blazing. "The fink didn't break up with me. I broke up with him."

Jerry smiled. "She speaks."

"She speaks because she's furious. The jerk was the same when we dated. I found out he was spreading rumors about the things we did."

Jerry cast a glance at the passenger seat. "What kind of things did the two of you do?"

"Nothing! That's the point. He went around telling everyone we did."

Jerry momentarily regretted warning the man about his illness. "So why would he say differently?"

Patti crossed her arms. "Because he's a guy and guys are jerks."

"I take exception to that."

"Okay, you're not a jerk, but most guys I went out with were. My mom was right."

"Brian seemed to think your mom liked him a lot. Claimed she planned your dates and even talked about the two of you getting married."

Patti swiped a strand of hair out of her face and crossed her arms once more. "Yeah, she liked him. He had a way about him that made parents like him. My mom thought he was the greatest. She liked him so much, she bribed me to go out with him. She'd tell me if I didn't go out with him, she wouldn't take me somewhere or do things she'd promised to do. The final straw came one day when Brian came over, and she started talking about our wedding. She said how we could get married in the backyard and talked about picking out a wedding gown. Brian and I had never even talked about marriage. That was it. I broke up with him that night."

"How'd your mom respond to that?"

"She was furious. But she eventually got over it. I never took another guy home after that. Not even after I graduated. I'd sneak around town like a schoolgirl afraid of getting caught."

"How did Brian take getting dumped?"

"He didn't kill me if that's what you're asking."

"Do you know who did?"

The anger left Patti's voice. "No, I just know it wasn't Brian."

"What about your parents or one of your brothers?"

"No. My family wasn't perfect, but they'd never do anything to harm me."

Good to know. "Brian said he saw you a couple days before you disappeared. You were in the Fox and Hound having dinner alone."

"I liked the food."

"He said he spoke with you and that you said you'd met someone that promised to take you away."

"It was a lie."

Jerry slid another glance at Patti. "Brian lied about that too?"

"No. I did. Brian stopped at my table and made some snide comment about my eating alone. He made sure to flash his wedding ring. I know he was just doing it to save face for my dumping him, but something about the way he was acting bothered me. So I lied and told him I'd met someone."

Jerry sighed. "He believed you. So much so, he told the police. That's probably why they stopped searching for you."

Patti faded in and out once more. "So my lies are what has kept me here?"

Maybe. Jerry spoke without looking at her. "They didn't help."

"That sucks." The implication was apparent in her tone.

"Yep."

Patti faded in and out several times and then disappeared completely. All for the best, as Jerry had nearly reached the restaurant. When Gunter materialized in the front seat, Jerry hid his relief. It was easy to see that the dog seemed to be taken with Patti. A small part of him worried that Gunter would follow her to the unknown.

Jerry reached for the dog and ruffled his fur. He wanted to tell Gunter he appreciated him hanging around, but this small token of affection was all he could muster at the moment.

He saw the sign for the restaurant, switched on his blinker, and turned in to the parking lot. His parents' car was parked near the building. Jerry wheeled the Durango around and backed into the space beside it. As he pressed the button to turn off the ignition, Jerry addressed Gunter. "We will be eating, so if you don't want to watch, you might want to stay out here."

Gunter yawned.

Jerry patted him on the head. "That's right, Buddy. Stay out here and sleep."

Jerry scanned the restaurant and saw his parents sitting in the far corner. Given the building was far from full, he knew they'd probably asked for the seat so they could talk to him in private. He passed a lady with a black lab service dog and was glad Gunter had stayed in the truck.

Jerry slid into a chair next to his mother, keeping his back to the wall. He skimmed the menu, decided on a burger and fries, and set the menu aside. "Have you guys ordered yet?"

His father shook his head. "Nope. Just got here a couple of moments ago."

The waitress approached and set a glass of water in front of Jerry. "Are you guys ready, or do you need a moment?"

They all ordered burgers and fries and the

waitress left. Lori cleared her throat to get Wayne's attention. His father nodded as a look passed between them. Jerry leaned back in the chair, waiting for whatever was about to take place.

Wayne intertwined his fingers and sat them on the table. "So, son, have you decided what comes next?"

"I was thinking about eating a burger."

His mother elbowed him. "You know what your father means."

"I have. But I'm not sure I can discuss it with you."

A frown tugged at his father's mouth. "I thought we'd gotten past the unpleasantness."

We'll soon find out. Jerry looked his father directly in the eye. "I've decided to use my gift to help people."

"That sounds like a good plan."

"Dead people."

To the man's credit, he didn't flinch. "Pays well, does it?"

Jerry smiled. "Probably not."

Wayne tapped his thumbs together. Jerry realized he too often did the same when struggling to collect his thoughts. The tapping stopped. "Do you still have the money Joseph left you?"

"Most of it." Jerry nodded toward the parking lot. "I paid cash for the ride, but I'd saved a lot more between the Marines and the department."

Lori tapped his forearm. "You've always been the frugal one."

"I guess Granny rubbed off on me."

His father took a sip from his glass. "In a lot of ways. So, these ghosts you're planning on helping, how are you going to find them?"

"I reckon they'll find me." Jerry shrugged. "They usually do."

Wayne rolled his neck. "I'm struggling with this."

"You're taking it better than I thought you would. It's true, though. I'm trying to help a childhood friend."

Lori gasped and clutched her chest. "Wait, is that why you were asking questions about Patricia O'Conner?"

"She's my current client." Shit, that sounded weird even to his own ears.

"That must've been who you were talking to in the driveway. Your father thought you were on something, but I told him that wasn't the case."

Wayne's face turned red. Jerry chuckled. "I assure you, my only vices are a few beers and the occasional Motrin."

Lori nodded toward his hand. "How is it?"

"Much better." Jerry flexed the fingers several times to drive home the point.

The waitress returned with the food, set their plates in front of them, and pulled a bottle of ketchup from her apron. "Does anyone need anything else?"

They all exchanged glances, then shook their heads.

"Okay, I'll check back with you in a bit."

Jerry heard a noise to his left and looked to see Gunter lying on the floor next to him, gnawing on a bloody bone. He looked up, saw his father watching, and smiled a sheepish smile.

"That dog is stressed."

Jerry snapped his head around, relaxing when he realized his mother was talking about the service dog who was staring in their direction. "How can you tell?"

"He's yawning. See, there he goes again."

Sure enough, the dog yawned and repositioned himself as he watched Gunter chew on the bone. "I thought yawning meant they were tired."

"Sometimes, but dogs aren't like people. They yawn to calm themselves down."

Jerry looked at Gunter and thought back to all the times the dog had yawned and he'd unwittingly assumed the K-9 to be tired. *Good to know*. Jerry felt his father staring and looked up. *Maybe I should tell him. Don't do it, Jerry. The guy is barely holding on as it is.*

His mother whispered, drawing their attention. "You're saying Patricia is dead, not missing?"

"I am. And I have to help find her body so she and her family can be at rest."

Lori gasped. "She was such a pretty lady. Are you sure she's dead?"

"I've spoken to her spirit. I just have to find her body so I can get the authorities involved."

Wayne finished chewing then asked the obvious question. "If you know she's dead and you're talking to her, why not just ask her where she's buried and be done with it?"

"Sounds logical, doesn't it?"

Wayne shook his hamburger at him. "Nothing about this conversation sounds logical."

Though his words were stressed, his tone showed he was trying to believe. Jerry plucked a fry from his plate before answering. "Unfortunately, it's not that easy. Patti's death must have been traumatic, as she can't or won't remember what happened to her."

Lori emitted another gasp. "Are you trying to say Patricia was murdered?"

"That's exactly what I'm saying. The trouble is until I can get Patti to remember, I'm not sure how to proceed."

"Go to the cops. Tell them who you are and they'll—"

Wayne cut her off. "They'll run your son out on a rail and make him out to be the laughingstock of the town."

"I'm afraid Dad's right. I'm not a cop anymore, so there won't be any professional courtesy." Jerry thought about telling him he might still have an in through Seltzer's little shell game but didn't want to worry them with the knowledge he'd been operating on a sliding scale of the law.

Wayne picked up a fry and purposely dropped it on the floor near where Gunter was lying. He watched the fry for several moments before looking up. He shrugged. "The way you keep looking down there, I thought maybe someone was there."

Jerry closed his eyes, gathering his courage. He opened them once more and met his father's gaze. "Do you really want to know?"

Jerry could see the inner struggle on his dad's face. "If I say no, your mother will pry it out of you later and tell me anyway. I guess you might as well spill it now."

"He's a police dog. His name's Gunter. He's a German shepherd. We worked for the same police force, and when he died, he came back and attached himself to me."

Lori clapped her hands together. "Oh, good, you've got yourself a dog."

Wayne was less enthusiastic. "I didn't think you liked dogs."

"I didn't think so either. But I think it was more because they didn't like me. Gunter's pretty cool and he's already helped me save a few lives since he's been here."

Wayne looked at the floor. "Never knew a dog who didn't like fries."

"I think it's because he's a ghost. I haven't seen him eat." Jerry decided to leave out the fact that the dog was currently chewing on a bloody bone.

"Wait, what about Marvin?"

Jerry turned toward his mother. "What about him?"

She seemed a bit undecided then forged on. "He told us you and he spoke and that he told you his little secret."

"You mean that he's not crazy."

"I wouldn't go that far," his father mumbled under his breath.

"Wayne, stop that right now. The boy and his uncle have finally found some peace. You, for one, should understand how that feels."

"It's okay, Mom. We did have a good talk and I'm definitely up for suggestions. Whatcha got?"

"I was just thinking that you could visit the detective that worked on Patricia's case."

"I've already told you they probably won't talk to me."

"They won't have to if you take Marvin along."

Jerry had to hand it to his mother; it wasn't a bad plan – provided Marvin was telling the truth when he said he could read everyone's mind. "It might just work."

Wayne looked at Lori and winked. "That's why I married the old girl. She has a brilliant head on her shoulders. That and she—"

"That's quite enough, Wayne."

Jerry ran his hand over his scalp, suddenly grateful he had not inherited his uncle's ability to read minds.

Chapter Twelve

Jerry waited for his parents' car to get out of sight before dialing Seltzer's number. The call connected and Seltzer's voice drifted through the speakers. "I was wondering when you were going to call. How was the reunion? You're not calling for bail money, are you?"

Jerry laughed. "I didn't shoot anyone if that's what you're asking."

"Probably for the best. Cops don't do well in prison."

"So I've heard."

"Did you call to ease my mind, or is there something I can do for you?"

"Maybe a little of both. It's been a good visit. Mended a lot of fences, plus I may have settled on a new career."

"You're going to get a job?" The disappointment was evident in the man's voice.

"Not a job. More like I've settled on a career path."

"I'm all ears."

That Seltzer knew and believed in Jerry's

abilities made the words come easy. "It was my uncle who suggested it."

"The uncle you can't stand?"

"Like I said, it's been a good trip. I'll fill you in on the details later."

"I can't wait. So tell me about this new direction."

"I ran into an old girlfriend. Before you jump to conclusions, she's dead."

"There's a joke in there somewhere, but for the life of me, I can't think of it."

"I'm pretty sure she was murdered."

"She can't tell you?"

"She either can't or doesn't want to remember."

"Must have been traumatic."

Jerry smiled. "You've been paying attention."

"Easy to keep up to speed when the subject is so fascinating."

"Anyway. It seems the police were given a false lead and, long story short, wrote her off as having skipped town."

"Meaning they stopped looking for her."

"Yes. Now I have to figure out how to find her body so the police can close the case and she and her family can have closure. I think she'll be at peace then."

"How are you going to find her remains if she won't tell you?"

Jerry rubbed his hand over his head. "I was

hoping you'd tell me."

When Seltzer grew quiet, Jerry pictured the man leaning back in his chair intently chomping his chewing gum. The chair creaked and Seltzer's voice floated through the speakers. "It'd be nice if you could look at the case files."

"I doubt they are going to allow me to see them, but I may have found a workaround."

"Do tell."

It was Jerry's turn to hesitate. "It seems my uncle is a mind reader."

"Jesus, Kid. What's in the water in Tennessee?"

"I know, right? Anyway, if I can talk to the detective and ask him key questions…"

"While his mouth is saying 'it's none of your business,' his mind will be telling all his secrets."

"That's the hope of it anyway."

"Send me what details you have on the woman. I'll run her name through the national database and see what shakes loose. Do it before you go to talk with the detective. Maybe if he gets a hit on the case, he will go over the files before you see him. It might help if the information is fresh in his head."

"Thanks, Sergeant."

"Anytime, son. Let me know what you find out and I'll do the same."

The dashboard went dark. Jerry picked up his phone, started a text message to Seltzer, and keyed in everything he knew about Patti. It wasn't much –

her name, birthday, and the fact that she had red hair and green eyes. He was going to add the freckles but decided against it. Those were most likely enhanced in his brain by a teenage boy's over-fertile imagination.

Jerry dialed Marvin's number.

"Jerry, my boy, I've been expecting your call."

"You were?"

"Your mother told me of her plan. I think it is a marvelous idea. Do you want me to meet you at the station, or would you prefer to pick me up?"

Good ol' Mom. Jerry checked the time. "How about I pick you up around two?"

"Ah, good boy. That will give your uncle time for a nice nap."

"I can make it later if you want?"

"Nope. Two will be just fine."

"Okay, see you in a bit."

Jerry had some time to kill, so he made his way to Cosby Highway, grabbed a few new towels for the bathroom, and sat in the Durango, twiddling his thumbs. After several moments of watching people come and go, Jerry moved to the far end of the parking lot, shut off the SUV, and leaned back, closing his eyes. If he was going to use his gift for this new purpose, he needed to figure out a way to channel his feelings. The problem was he was used to using his feelings to prevent crimes. In Patti's case, the crime had already been committed.

Okay, think like a criminal. How would you do it if you wanted to dispose of a body? The river? Probably not. If the killer tossed her in the river, someone would have discovered her body by now. Not if they weighted it down. Shit. Okay, that is the most obvious solution, but what else? Concrete. That's a good one. Jerry wondered if there was any way of finding out what construction projects were completed within a few days of when Patti went missing.

He opened his eyes, surveying his surroundings. *Jesus, Jerry, you're a stone's throw from the woods no matter what direction you turn. Patti's killer could have tossed her body anywhere in the mountains and the animals would've done the rest.*

Gunter's ears twitched. He jumped up and moved to the back seat. A second later, Granny appeared in the seat the dog had just vacated. "That's a pretty morbid thought."

Jerry smiled. "Just walking through the possibilities."

"Have you been back to see your brother?"

Jerry sighed. "No."

"Now is as good of a time as any."

Jerry checked the clock on the dashboard. "Fine, I'll go now. I won't be able to stay long, as I'm going to pick up Marvin at two."

His grandmother's face lit up. "I'm so glad the two of you mended fences."

"We would have done so a lot sooner if you had let me in on the big secret."

Her smile waned. "It's not my place to lead you on your journey. This is your path, Jerry. It's up to you to pick your way."

Jerry sighed. "Alright, how about a little nudge every now and then?"

"I already have." She disappeared before Jerry could ask what she meant.

He felt a cool breeze. A second later, Patti sat in the passenger seat. Jerry was beginning to wonder if the seat was a vortex to the other world. "Welcome back."

Patti spoke without looking in his direction. "I'm not in the water."

Jerry ran a hand over his head and wondered how many times his thoughts had been heard.

"I wasn't spying. I just felt you thinking about me and tuned in."

Jerry pressed his fingers to his temples. *Marilyn Monroe*. Patti laughed. Jerry realized it was the first time he'd heard her do so. He started the Durango and headed toward the cemetery. "Knowing you're not in the water is helpful. It will keep us from wasting our time dredging the river."

"They already did that. I remember standing by my father on the riverbank as he watched them."

"Can you recall anything else about what happened to you?"

"I remember a bell."

Jerry cocked his head. "What kind of bell?"

Patti's image faded in and out several times. "I don't know. I just remember hearing one. There's something else."

Jerry glanced at Patti as he turned onto Mineral Street. "What?"

"He hurt me, Jerry. He hurt me really bad."

"I'm sorry, Patti." Whether she heard him or not, he didn't know. Because when he looked again, she was gone. Jerry wondered if her disappearance was from her admission or because he had once again turned in to Union Cemetery.

Gunter left the vehicle before Jerry parked, racing along with his nose to the ground. Jerry walked to Joseph's grave and shoved his hands into his pockets, waiting for his brother to appear. He didn't have to wait long.

"I wasn't sure if you were going to come back before you left town."

Jerry kicked at the dirt. "Neither was I."

"Are you still mad at me?"

"No."

"How's your hand?"

Jerry flexed his fingers inside his pocket. "Who told you?"

"I was there."

"Do me a favor. Next time you see that I'm about to do something stupid, stop me."

"Granny said I shouldn't get involved."

"My life. My rules. If you think I need an intervention, feel free to intervene."

"You were pretty angry. Do you really think you would have listened to me?"

"Probably not. But you could've tried. You owed me that."

"Jesus, Jerry and Joseph, every time the two of you get together, all you do is squabble."

Jerry turned to his grandmother. "I didn't think you liked coming here."

His grandmother pointed a gnarled finger at them. "Someone has to keep the two of you in line. Besides, while the two of you are getting into it, that dog of yours is digging up the cemetery."

Jerry looked to where she was pointing. Sure enough, Gunter was paws deep in the dirt, digging a hole in front of a headstone. *Shit!* Jerry sprinted off, calling Gunter's name as he ran. The dog paid him no mind while tearing at the dirt as if going after a buried treasure.

Jerry remembered the bone Gunter was chewing on at lunch and his stomach clenched. "Gunter, cease!"

The dog kept digging.

"Gunter, stop!"

No response.

Jerry reached for him and grabbed a handful of fur. Gunter turned on him and sank his teeth into

Jerry's arm. "Ow, shit, dog. What's your problem?"

Instantly, the dog's demeanor changed. Gunter whined an apologetic whine, wiggling and licking Jerry's face. Jerry moved the dog aside, checked his arm, and saw two dots of blood where the K-9's teeth had punctured the skin. *Shit!* Jerry wiped the blood away with his other hand.

"Please tell me you're up to date on your rabies shot. What's with all the digging anyway?" Jerry remembered the bone. "Never mind. I don't want to know."

Gunter lay down in front of the stone.

"Move it, dog."

Gunter popped up and backed out of the way as Jerry pushed the dirt back in place with the toe of his boot. He looked at the headstone, reading the inscription. "Sorry, Mrs. Emery."

Having patched the dirt, Jerry started back toward his brother's grave. He'd walked several feet before realizing Gunter was not at his side. He turned and slapped his hand to his outer thigh. "Gunter, come!"

The dog remained where he was.

Jerry slapped his leg, his patience waning. "Gunter, COME!"

Gunter started forward then disappeared.

"Yeah, well, good riddance!" Jerry bypassed Joseph's grave and returned to the Durango, where he poured the contents of a bottle of water over his arm.

Joseph appeared at his side. "Nice ride."

"Thanks."

"What's with the attitude?"

"You're a ghost. Do you think ghost dogs can have rabies?"

Joseph laughed. "You know, for a Marine, you're kind of a wimp."

"I'm not a wimp. The friggin' dog bit me and he's dead. Put yourself in my place."

Joseph raised an eyebrow. "I'd love to. And it's your own fault for getting in his way."

"In his way? The dog was in the process of desecrating a grave." Jerry tossed the empty water bottle into the cab. "Listen, I'm sorry, but I've got someplace I have to be. I doubt I will get out here again before I leave."

Joseph heaved a heavy sigh.

"Don't be like that. You know as well as I do that we are not limited to talking here."

Joseph opened his mouth as if to reply and closed it once again.

"I'll be seeing you, Joseph."

Joseph gave a small nod. "Take care of yourself, big brother."

Chapter Thirteen

The detective who had worked Patti's case agreed to see them so quickly that Jerry knew Seltzer's plan had worked. Jerry and Marvin followed Detective Rowland into a small office, where he waved them to be seated as he closed the door. The man had "cop" written all over him, from the cocky swagger to the way his eyes logged in every detail of his unexpected guest.

Rowland took a seat behind the desk and intertwined his fingers. "Trooper McNeal, I'm seeing you out of professional courtesy. With that said, I wasn't under the impression state police worked on missing persons cases."

Jerry leaned back in his chair. "I'm afraid there's been a slight misunderstanding. I'm not here on official business. Patti was a friend. I was in town, and to be honest, I wasn't aware she was missing until two days ago."

"So, instead of coming to see me first, you ordered a background check."

Jerry decided to keep Seltzer's name out of the mix. He leaned forward and purposely lowered his voice. "A friend in the department owed me a favor. I told him we'd call it square if he did this for me."

Detective Rowland's eye twitched. "Did you find what you were looking for?"

Jerry hadn't spoken to Seltzer yet. He shook his head. "I was hoping you could read me in on what you found. I planned on stopping by and chatting with Patti's parents and figured I could tell them if you have any new leads."

Another eye twitch. "There aren't any new leads because we consider it a closed case. The woman ran off with a boyfriend."

"That doesn't sound like the Patti I knew."

"You've been gone a long time. People change."

"Patti was close to her mother. Don't you find it odd she hasn't so much as sent a Christmas card?"

"I hear the mother was controlling. Maybe Patricia grew tired of it."

Jerry leaned back in his chair once more. "Or, maybe something happened to her to keep her from sending that card."

"Something like?"

Jerry glanced at his uncle before answering. "Like maybe Patti was murdered, and you gave up the search for her body too soon."

"I assure you our police department is most adept at conducting a search. Why, we even dredged the river to appease her family. You said you're going to visit them. Are you sure that's such a wise thing to do? It's been five years. Why stir things up again when you have no proof to back up your suspicions?"

Jerry's proof had joined them the moment they'd begun speaking. The only problem was he and Marvin were the only ones who could see her. "So you'll not give me the courtesy of looking at the file?"

Rowland picked up the folder and placed it on the counter behind him. "I don't see where that would do anyone any good."

Jerry looked at Marvin. "Well, I guess there's no use beating a dead horse."

Rowland smiled a triumphant smile. "Especially when the horse isn't dead."

Jerry looked at Marvin. "Ready, Uncle?"

Marvin pushed off from the chair. "Yep. Heard all I needed to hear."

Jerry waited until they were inside the Durango before speaking. "Well?"

"He's not hiding anything other than the fact that he wrote Patti off the moment your friend Brian told him Patti had run off with her boyfriend. He never gave the case another thought until today when he saw someone was snooping around. It scared him. He's been going through the files all day wondering if he missed something."

Patti piped up from the back seat. "Besides the fact that I was murdered?"

Jerry looked in the mirror. "Patti, Uncle Marvin. Marvin, this is Patti."

Marvin smacked his leg. "The man would have crapped his pants if he knew you were sitting on his desk."

"I wish I knew how to let him see me. Jerry, where's your dog?"

"Don't know. I haven't seen him since I left the cemetery. Probably knows I'm pissed at him for biting me."

Marvin grabbed Jerry's arm. "Is that what that is? Dog bites are nothing to fool around with. You'd better go get it looked at before it gets infected."

Jerry rolled his neck. It wasn't that the wound was all that bad. It was that it had been inflicted by a ghost dog. "I can't have it checked. Dog bites are an automatic report. I go in, they will be looking for a dog. While they won't find Gunter, they might find some other stray and punish him for nothing. I'll stop on the way home and get some peroxide. It'll be fine."

"Nonsense. You come inside when we get to the cabin and let Stella fix you up."

She'd like that.

"Of course she would. She likes you."

Abcdefghijklmnop

"What the devil are you doing?"

"Getting you out of my mind. Turn off whatever it is you're doing."

Patti leaned in between them and Jerry was grateful for the distraction. "Now what?"

Jerry shifted into drive and pushed on the gas pedal. "Now I take my uncle home."

***

Seltzer had phoned while Jerry was inside the cabin. Rather than having him read off the whole report, Jerry asked him to email it so he could print it off from Marvin's computer. He now sat on the deck with a can of Budweiser, looking over the report while Patti wandered the yard picking dandelions.

Jerry took a sip of beer and reread the report. Patti went missing on July 31, 2018. Something about that date nagged at him. *Come on, Jerry, what are you missing?* It was right there. He knew it.

Sammy ran up the stairs with a bone in his mouth. Jerry watched as the dog left a trail of dirt in his wake. Jerry shook his head. What was it with dogs and digging?

Sammy lowered to the deck and began gnawing on the bone.

Shit! "Marvin!" Jerry scrambled from the chair and hurried inside.

Marvin had obviously been snoozing in the recliner and was in the process of lowering the foot of the chair. "What's on your mind, boy?"

"Do you know anyone who works at the cemetery?"

"I might. What's got you so riled?"

Jerry almost told him to read his mind but decided against it. The less his uncle knew what was going on inside his brain, the better. "Sarah D. Emery died July 27, 2018. I need to know what day she was buried."

"Mind telling me why?"

"Because if my hunch is right, and I think it is, I think Patti's killer is a very smart man. I think he covered up his crime by burying Patti in the same grave. The dirt would have already been fresh, therefore it wouldn't have taken much time to dig far enough to cover the body."

Marvin went in search of a number to call. Jerry returned to the deck, aiming to call out to Patti, and found her waiting for him. He looked over the rail. "Not thinking of jumping, are you?"

She sighed. "Wouldn't do any good."

"I think I found something."

She faced him and waited for him to speak.

"I thought you were staying out of the cemetery because you didn't think you belonged. But that wasn't the case, was it? You didn't want to go in there because you didn't want to remember what happened to you there."

She was trembling and he saw tears well in her eyes.

"Is that where it happened, or did you just see him burying your body?"

"Both." She rubbed at her arms but let her tears flow untouched. "He had a van. There were bells."

"You mentioned the bells before. What kind of bells?"

"On the radio, maybe. A song with bells."

"What else do you remember?"

"He did awful things to me, Jerry." Her voice trembled as she spoke.

"It's alright, Patti. You don't have to go into detail just yet. Do you know how he killed you?"

"He strangled me. He was smiling the whole time. The last thing I heard was those damn bells." As she spoke, a vicious purple bruise appeared around her throat.

"Did you see him bury your body?"

Her brow furrowed. "I think so."

"Do you remember what he looked like?"

She shook her head.

"Anything, Patti. Any little detail that will help us nail the bastard that did this to you."

"I just remember the bells."

Marvin came out onto the deck. "Your hunch was right. Sarah died on July 27th and was buried the morning of the 31st. Someone with a shovel could have easily loosened the dirt enough to place another body in the grave. Good work, Jerry."

Patti spoke first. "A lot of good knowing is going to do. You heard the detective. He thinks I'm missing. Do you really think he will buy into it enough to exhume the grave?"

"The grave is already disturbed. Gunter saw to that." Jerry directed his next comment to Patti. "We're going to have to tell your parents. If I call Rowland, he's likely to blow me off again. But if your parents were to contact him and tell him they received an anonymous tip, he's going to have to act. All we have to do is get Rowland curious enough to go have a look. If he's spooked enough to think that someone else has already been digging around, that might just be the catalyst to get him to go to Sarah's family and ask permission. He shouldn't need a warrant as he won't have to dig deep enough to disturb her casket."

Patti wrung her hands. "This is going to devastate my parents."

"This is going to give them closure," Jerry corrected.

***

Jerry drove the length of North Street several times before Patti finally gathered enough courage to allow him to pull into the driveway. Both the house and the property it sat on looked as sad as the daughter that had once lived there. "Are you ready to do this, Patti?"

"I can't think of any other way."

Jerry shut the engine off. "Neither can I. It won't be easy."

"I know."

Jerry approached the door with Patti at his side. He rang the doorbell and waited.

Patti's mom answered. An aura of sadness hung over the woman as she narrowed her eyes at him. "Whatever you're selling, we ain't buying."

Jerry reached for the door as the woman pushed it closed, catching his injured hand between the door and the jamb. Shit!

Mrs. O'Conner opened the door enough for Jerry to pull his hand out, and he managed to slip his foot in the opening before she could close it again. He flexed his fingers several times to make sure nothing was broken.

Mrs. O'Conner was unconcerned over the pain she'd inflicted. "Ronnie, bring the gun!"

Jerry looked at Patti. "Mrs. O'Conner, it's me, Jerry McNeal. I used to date your daughter. I have news for you."

The door flew open. "You have news about Patricia?"

Jerry felt bad about giving the woman false hope, but it was all he could think of to get her attention. "Please, if I can just come inside so we can talk."

"I guess." She stepped back just as her husband arrived with a shotgun. "He says he has news about Patricia."

Ronnie lowered the gun. "What kind of news?"

"I don't know. He hasn't bothered to tell me yet."

Jerry felt his jaw clench and ran his hand over his

head. "Please, if we can just sit for a moment."

Ronnie set the shotgun aside, took his wife by the arm, and led her to the couch. He motioned Jerry to sit then took a seat on the sofa beside his wife. "You said you have some news about our little girl?"

"I do, but I'm afraid it's not the news you were hoping for."

Patti's mother burst into tears. Ronnie patted her leg to comfort her. "There there, Rachel, we both knew this was a possibility. Are you with the police department, then?"

"No, sir, I am a friend of your daughter."

"This was the boy from school. The one that wanted to soil Patricia's reputation."

Jerry held his tongue.

"I don't understand. If you're not with the department, how do you know what happened to Patricia?"

Jerry took in a breath. "Because she told me. I can speak with the dead."

Rachel's cries turned into hysterical sobs, and for a moment, Ronnie looked as though he regretted leaving the shotgun by the door. His face turned crimson, and he narrowed his eyes. "How dare you come here and prey on our grief! Get out now, before I call the cops. Better yet, get out before I shoot you myself."

Jerry addressed Rachel. "The day Patti disappeared, she came to the house and did a load of laundry. You had eaten a pomegranate right before she arrived and dripped some of the juice from the seeds onto your white shirt. You asked her to put the shirt in the wash with her stuff in hopes that it wouldn't stain."

Rachel's eyes grew wide. "How do you know about that? I never told anyone."

"Patti told me."

Ronnie wasn't convinced. "She could have told you that before she disappeared."

Jerry directed his comment to Patti's father. "She could have, but she didn't."

Patti moved to the arm of the couch and sat next to her father.

Jerry repeated her words. "It was misting rain the day they dredged the river. On your way down the riverbank, you slipped in the mud. As you got up, you plucked a dandelion and placed it into your left pants pocket. Patti said she used to pick them for you whenever you took her to the river, and you would always put them in your front left pants pocket. After the men finished dredging the river, you hung around, watching the water flow past. Before you left, you tossed the flower in the river and prayed that your daughter was still alive and that wherever she was, she was picking flowers."

Ronnie blinked back tears. "How do you know that?"

Jerry smiled. "Patti was standing beside you the

whole time you thought you were alone. She's sitting beside you right now."

"Patricia's here?" It was Rachel who spoke.

"She is."

"Is she in any pain?"

Jerry shook his head. "Not anymore."

Rachel plucked a Kleenex from the box beside her and blew her nose. "We knew you didn't run away. We knew you wouldn't do that to us."

"She said to tell you she didn't run away and wants me to tell you we know where her body is." Jerry took a breath to allow his words to sink in.

Ronnie pushed off from the couch. "Where is she? We'll go get her."

Jerry held up his hands. "Patti's spirit is here. She's been here all along. Believe me when I tell you I am as eager to recover her body as you are, but that's the tricky part."

Ronnie lowered back to the couch. "Tricky, how?"

"Patti's body is buried in a shallow grave in Union Cemetery. She shares the grave with a woman by the name of Sarah D. Emery." Jerry held up his hand to let them know he wasn't finished. "Patti was kidnapped and assaulted before being strangled to death. Sarah was buried the day Patti was killed. She was already in the ground before anyone started looking for her. Even if they had searched the cemetery, no one would have looked twice at the grave."

Ronnie looked from side to side. "Patti, it's Dad. Can you hear me?"

Jerry pointed to where Patti was sitting. "She can."

"Who did this to you? Give me a name and I'll see that he pays."

"Sir, I fully understand your need for revenge, but Patti doesn't know. She remembers enough to know she didn't know the man but not enough to give a description of her assailant. The only thing she can remember is bells – possibly music with bells in it."

Rachel looked toward the end of the couch, a river of tears streaming down her face. "Are you sure she isn't in any pain?"

"Nothing hurts if that is what you mean. She's been in limbo for a long time, but she seems to be more at ease now that you know. I believe she will be more at peace once her physical body is properly buried."

Ronnie blew his nose into his handkerchief then dabbed the corners of his eyes. "You said getting her body will be tricky. Why can't we tell the police what you just told us?"

Jerry wished it were that easy. "I spoke with the detective today. That was before I'd figured out where Patti's body was. The man is convinced Patti skipped town."

"Then we'll dig her up ourselves."

Rachel nodded her agreement.

"No, I think there's a better way. Call the detective the first thing in the morning. Tell him you received an anonymous tip in the middle of the night telling you where to find your daughter's body."

"Won't they check our phone records?"

"Probably, but I don't think it will happen until after they find her remains. By then, it won't matter."

"What if they find out you told us? Won't they suspect you?"

"Perhaps. Don't worry about me. I have people that know what I'm capable of and will vouch for my whereabouts on the day Patti went missing." Jerry stood. "I'm going to be going now. I'm very sorry for your loss."

Ronnie clutched his wife's hand. "Is Patti going with you?"

"No, she's going to stay with you for now. Once she is properly buried, her spirit will be at rest, and she will be free to come and go as she pleases."

"Will you be there when they dig?"

Jerry pulled a small notebook from his pocket and jotted down his full name and cell number. He handed the paper to Ronnie. "I'll be leaving town soon, but if you need anything, give me a call, and I'll see what I can do."

Ronnie's hand trembled as he pocketed the

paper. "Thank you, Mr. McNeal, for everything. I don't know how to repay you."

Jerry waved him off. "There's no need to pay me. Just knowing everyone is getting closure is payment enough."

Chapter Fourteen

Jerry left the O'Conners with a deep feeling of satisfaction. That he could give the family closure warmed his heart. What didn't sit well was that he hadn't seen Gunter since the incident at the cemetery. He flexed his hand and felt it in his forearm. Since he'd been in Tennessee, he'd busted his knuckles, got bitten by a frenzied ghost, and had a door slammed on the same hand. Maybe there was something to be said about having bad luck after breaking the mirror.

Jerry shook off the thought. Breaking that mirror wasn't the problem. It was just all a series of bad choices. Gunter didn't attack him. Dead or alive, the dog was a trained K-9 police officer and Jerry had disturbed him when he was working. *Jesus, McNeal, you're lucky the dog didn't tear your whole arm off.* Jerry also had to admit he'd screwed up. The hand in the door was his own fault as well. Even rookies knew enough to utilize their foot to prevent a door from slamming in their face. *Been off the job a handful of weeks, and you're already getting soft. Better get a grip on things, McNeal.*

Jerry thought of Patti as he listened to the rumble of the engine echoing through the mountains. *As soon as they get her body, there's going to be a funeral.* He didn't like funerals – never had. Mostly because while people stood around mourning the dead, he was trying not to look out of place watching the ghost of the person being mourned, listening to everything being said about them. Most of the time, the spirit would wander around trying to comfort the funeral-goers. But on occasion, someone would unwittingly insult the deceased. Jerry found it difficult to keep a straight face when a pissed-off ghost insisted on poking fun at all who dared comment on the way his or her body was preserved. Though under the circumstances, he didn't foresee anyone viewing the body at Patti's funeral, the truth of the matter was he preferred to think of her happily wandering through the yard in search of dandelions than in a box covered in dirt.

If I'm not here, they won't expect me to attend. Now that Patti's parents knew where to find her body, there was no reason for him to stay. *I'll leave in the morning.*

Deciding to leave was the easy part – knowing where to go next proved to be more difficult. His parents had asked him to visit, but it was much too soon. If he showed up now, he would appear desperate or, even worse, not confident with the choice he'd made. No, he would wait until later –

plan the visit over a holiday, where it would feel more natural. Okay, so he knew where not to go. One state down.

Something black at the side of the road ahead of him caught his attention. Jerry pressed the brakes as a mother bear and three cubs crossed the road about thirty feet in front of his Durango. He glanced at the passenger seat to gauge Gunter's reaction and sighed.

Jerry checked the time, then used the buttons on the steering wheel to call Savannah.

"No, you can't have your cat back."

"Good. I don't miss the cat hair."

"Now that we have that settled, what's up? How's the cabin? How did the reunion go?"

"I'm watching a mother and cubs not too far from the turnoff to the cabin." Jerry waited for the bears to clear then pressed on the gas.

"Oh, man, I never get that lucky. How many cubs?"

"Three. The reunion was good. I wanted to let you know I'm leaving in the morning. And I promise to leave the cabin better than I found it."

"You should hang around. Alex and I will be up next weekend. You'd have to move to the couch, but you're welcome to stay."

A part of him wanted to hang around so that he could see their faces when they saw the changes he made to the bathroom. "I'd love to, but you know how it is. Places to go and people to save."

"You're taking the ghost with you, right?"

Jerry instantly pictured Gunter then remembered he'd told her about Patti. "I think she's staying local, but I don't think she will find her way back to the cabin after I'm gone."

"Are you sure? Because I don't want to have to explain to Alex that I'm seeing another woman."

Jerry chuckled as he turned to go up the mountain. "Hey, remember how she wouldn't go into the cemetery? It was because that was where she was murdered." Jerry went on to tell Savannah about the events of the past few days.

"That's some scary shit!"

"I'm thinking this is my calling. It feels right, like it's what I'm supposed to be doing."

"If you want to solve murders, why not just join the police force and become a detective?"

"Because there would be rules. I don't seem to do well with those."

"So where do you go from here?"

"The only thing I know is where I don't go."

"Where's that?"

"Florida. I go down there now, and my mom will try to get me to move in. I may be an old soul, but I'm pretty sure I'm still too young for The Villages."

She laughed. "I think you're right. Okay, Florida's out. That leaves forty-nine states to choose from."

"Forty-eight. I can't drive to Hawaii."

"Sounds like a fun problem to have. Listen, Alex is calling in, so I have to go. If you find yourself in our neighborhood, make sure to stop by and say hello."

"Will do." Jerry had no sooner said the words when the call was lost and he was once again alone with his thoughts. Weird that it bothered him – he'd never minded being alone before. It dawned on him he hadn't lived alone for some time. Though Cat had been a pain in the ass, the feline had helped him climb out of the darkness on occasion.

Now, without Gunter to keep him company, the solitude of the cabin felt less welcoming. Jerry took a Motrin for his hand and decided to call it an early night. Too early, perhaps, as sleep wouldn't come. He lay there with his hands stretched over his head, staring into the darkness. He'd opened the bedroom window, enjoying the cool mountain air as he listened to the crickets' serenade, and sifted through the events of the last few days. His grandmother had known the whereabouts of Patti's remains, a deduction made obvious by the fact that she kept pushing him to go to the cemetery. Even Joseph had acted as if he'd wanted to say more but hadn't because of the so-called code of the dead. He'd have to have a talk with them and figure out a way to convince them to be more forthcoming.

He'd hated to discover that Patti was dead but

was grateful he was able to help her and her family find closure. He'd come so close to not coming, and if he hadn't, he wouldn't have found his way back to his family. It dawned on him that his grandmother had known about Patti even before he arrived as she'd told him he needed to help her. Patti had been dead for five years. If he would have returned earlier, would he have been able to help her sooner? He let that guilt go. How would he have found her if it wasn't for Gunter? That revelation bothered him as he hadn't seen the dog since the incident by the grave. Was that why Gunter had been sent to him, to help find Patti's body? Was that why the dog was missing because his job here was done? He had so many questions floating around in his head, sleep was the last thing on his mind.

Jerry was just about to get up when he heard an owl hoot in the distance. A few seconds later, the call was answered by one further away.

A memory from his childhood floated to mind. Jerry recalled lying in bed listening to the owls calling to one another from nearby trees. They'd start off close to the house, their hoots so loud, they sounded as if the birds sat right outside the window ledge. More than once, he sat staring out into the darkness, hoping to get a glimpse of one of the birds. Then one night he shined a flashlight in the tree and spooked one of the owls who gathered its wings, screeching his fury as he flew away. In the days that followed, the nights were silent and Jerry realized he greatly missed hearing the comforting hoots. He'd prayed for over a week, asking God to send the bird back, promising if he did, he would let him sing in peace.

Then one night, the owl returned, and Jerry once again found comfort in the nightly serenade. Some people counted sheep. Jerry preferred hoots. Though the garage he'd rented in Pennsylvania was nestled in the trees, he couldn't recall the last time he'd heard an owl. As he lay listening to his visitor, Jerry's tension eased and sleep finally found him.

***

While Jerry still planned on leaving, he had no idea where he was going and was in no hurry to get on the road. He spent the morning cleaning the cabin – washing and drying the sheets and returning them to the bed. He relocated the tattered towels to the laundry closet and hung the new ones in the bathroom. He was pleased with the transformation. Oh, to be a fly on the wall when Savannah and Alex entered and saw their newly updated space. Just picturing their excitement made him almost happy he'd busted the mirror. Jerry flexed his still tender fingers. *Almost.*

Jerry's cell rang. He checked the time and saw it was just after eleven in the morning – the caller ID showed a Tennessee number, so he answered. "Hello?"

"Mr. McNeal, this is Ronnie O'Conner. I just wanted to let you know they've uncovered Patti's remains."

Jerry rocked back on his heels. "These Tennessee boys work fast. I'm impressed."

"We can give my wife credit for that. A couple of hours after you left, she was so upset she insisted we call the police station and demanded they have Detective Rowland contact us. When he called, she did like you said and told them she'd gotten a call about Patti. Beings she was so upset, I didn't think there was no harm in making the call early. Figured it would sound more believable."

"You're probably right about that."

"Anyhow, from the sound of it, Detective Rowland took a flashlight and went out in the middle of the night to have himself a look. When he called, he said it looked like someone had already been digging. I figured that was you but didn't tell him that. He called in his forensic team and we – her mother, brothers and me – were there when they found her this morning. I have to tell you it was hard seeing our baby girl like that, but the wife and I take comfort in what you said about her not being in any pain. I know you said there's no need to repay you, but I thought to tell you this. One of the boys, his wife's gonna have a baby. They're going to have one of those x-ray things next week that tell 'em what the baby's going to be. And, well, if it's a boy, they done plan on naming him Jerry after the man that brought their sister home."

As Jerry searched for a proper response, Patti appeared. She was smiling. "I'd be honored to share my name."

"We plan on having a small family ceremony and giving Patti a proper burial as soon as they release her remains to us. You're welcome to join us."

"I appreciate the offer, but I've already said my goodbyes to Patti." Or would as soon as he ended the call.

Patti waved her hands. "Tell him not to invite Brian."

"Mr. O'Conner?"

"Yes."

"It's up to you, but I wouldn't invite Brian McCampbell. Patti didn't like the guy as much as everyone thought." Jerry considered telling the man that Brian was the reason the police stopped looking for their daughter, but Patti had a hand in that, and the man would soon have enough to worry about without adding to it.

"Good to know. Thank you again for everything you've done for our family."

"Glad to be of help, sir." Jerry ended the call and looked for Patti. He found her sitting on the front porch petting Gunter. Seeing them together was both a relief and cause for concern. "Be careful. He'll tear your arm off."

As Jerry came out onto the porch, Gunter moved away from Patti and lowered into a crouch, resting his head on his paws.

Jerry sat on the swing. Patti pressed her shoulder into his. The weight against him felt solid – too solid to be anything but real. Jerry sighed.

"Don't be so hard on him, Jerry. He feels bad for what he did. He was trying to tell you where I was. He didn't mean to hurt you."

To Gunter's credit, the dog did look rather contrite.

"He didn't hurt me. Not really. I may have been a bit freaked out for a minute." Jerry thought back to when he was trying to protect Savannah, and Manning had gotten in the way. In that moment, he'd thought about shooting the man himself. "It was my fault for getting in his way. Without him, we might never have found your body."

Gunter lifted his head and cocked it to the side as if to ask if that was an apology.

"You're a good boy, Gunter. You did good."

At the sound of his name, Gunter popped up and put his paws on Jerry's chest while licking his face.

Patti smiled. "You're doing pretty good for someone who doesn't like dogs."

"I like dogs." Jerry laughed. "Okay, that might be a stretch. But I like this dog."

"And he likes you."

Jerry glanced at Patti. "He seems to be rather

taken with you as well."

"Jerry McNeal, are you jealous?"

"No. Maybe."

Patti laughed a carefree laugh. "This dog might like other people. But he is committed to you. You don't have to worry about him going anywhere. You're stuck with him."

The knowledge warmed his heart. There was a time when Jerry wanted nothing more than to be rid of the dog. That time had long passed. Jerry's cell phone rang. He saw the call was from Max and declined the call.

Patti frowned. "You're not going to answer?"

"I'll call her back in a bit." He enjoyed sitting next to Patti and didn't want to risk her disappearing if he took the call. Though her energy felt lighter, something still didn't feel quite right. "I thought your energy would feel more at peace after they found your body."

Jerry's cell rang. He pulled the phone from his pocket, saw it was Max and started to silence it once again. Patti placed her hand on his and shook her head. "You need to help us, Jerry. You're the only one."

*Join Jerry McNeal and his ghostly
K-9 partner as they put their gifts to good use in:*

Port Hope
Book 5 in the Jerry McNeal series.

Available May 27, 2022 on Amazon Kindle:

https://www.amazon.com/gp/product/B09V3LQ8WM/ref=dbs_a_def_rwt_bibl_vppi_i4

Please help me by leaving a review!

**Enjoy what you read? Please tell
EVERYONE!**

About the Author

Born in Kentucky, Sherry got her start in writing by pledging to write a happy ending to a good friend who was going through some really tough times. The story surprised her by taking over and practically writing itself. What started off as a way to make her friend smile started her on a journey that would forever change her life. Sherry readily admits to hearing voices and is convinced that being married to her best friend for forty-one-plus years goes a long way in helping her write happily-ever-afters.

Sherry resides in Michigan and spends most of her time writing from her home office, traveling to book signing events, and giving lectures on the Orphan Trains.

Made in the USA
Coppell, TX
23 March 2023